ROGUE COVEN

WITCHIN' IMPOSSIBLE COZY MYSTERIES

RENEE GEORGE

BARKSIDE OF THE MOON PRESS

Rogue Coven: Witchin' Impossible Cozy Mysteries Book 2

2nd Edition

Publisher: Barkside of the Moon Press

Print Date: 1/1/2019

ISBN: 978-1-947177-25-3

Dedication

For Love.

Because what could be more important.

ACKNOWLEDGMENTS

A special THANK YOU to the fabulous Robyn Peterman, an awesomely funny writer and my favorite cookie, for allowing me the privilege to write in her world and then turning around allowing me to turn this series into my own world. I love your guts, woman!!

Also, I must thank my BFF and critique partner Michele Bardsley. You complete me! And to my sister Robbin, whom I would be completely lost without.

To my Rebels, you all RAWK! You keep me going every day with your support. I love you to the moon and back.

To my fans, I would not be anything without you. Seriously. If you keep reading, I'll keep writing! Thank you. Thank you. Thank you. If I were reviewing you all, you would get five-gazillion stars and a million-gazillion smooches.

Oh! And lest I forget, thank you strong, black coffee. Without you, I couldn't get out of bed in the morning, let alone write a single word.

Rogue witches. Halloween Pranks. Dead body. A hellmouth at the four-way between Main Street and Bliss. For Police Chief Haze Kinsey, it's just another day in Paradise Falls.

In the paranormal town of Paradise Falls, witch Hazel Kinsey is settling into her new job as police chief and as the mate of hunky werebear Ford Baylor.

Unfortunately, Halloween in Paradise Falls means enduring yet another year of prank wars between the witches and the Shifters. She must tolerate the annoying shenanigans until one trick turns out to be a real killer.

Now Hazel has to solve the murder, protect her mate from rampant clown attacks, host a Halloween party for her squirrel familiar, and oh yeah, shut down the hellmouth that's appeared in the middle of town.

CHAPTER 1

"**P**uhleassssse, Hazel!" my squirrel familiar Tizzy said. Her tiny red-furred fingers were clasped together, and she was down on her little knees, blinking up at me with her large, lovely brown eyes. "It'll be All Hallows Eve in ten days. You know, the Devil's night, Hallowtide, *Nos Calan Gaeaf.*"

I gave her a *WTF* look.

She threw her paws up in the air, her voice going higher pitched. "You're right, that Celtic reference was obscure even for me." She jumped from the kitchen counter, did a quick bounce on a diner stool, and landed with a skid across the marble center island. She stirred my coffee with one finger and cast her determined gaze up at me. "The point I'm trying to make is that Halloween is right around the corner! It's only a week away. I really need a decision from you."

I flicked her paw away from my cup. "You're not turning our home into a haunted house."

Her chin dropped down to her chest, and her nose twitched. "You suck."

"I know, Tizzy. And I'm a terrible witch," I said, borrowing one of her favorite lines. Mostly because it was entirely true. I'd spent seventeen years avoiding my abilities while hiding in the human world as an FBI agent. Now that I was back in my hometown of Paradise Falls, and I could use my witchcraft freely, I found I still preferred my 9 MM pistol to magic.

She stretched her arms wide with excitement as she went up on her tiny toes. "We could have smoke machines, cobwebs strung all over, bowls of eyeballs and guts, and spiders," she chirped. "Lots of big, fat, hairy spiders!" I must have gasped because she wiggled her fingers at me and said, "Unless that's a deal-breaker." She waved her hands in front of her chest. "Then no spiders."

"This is the first time in a very long time since we've had a real home, Tiz. We're not turning it into a sideshow attraction." Besides, the yearly prank wars between the witches and the shifters had started, and I didn't want to paint a big old "Toilet Paper Me" sign on my house. I pointed at my persistent familiar. "I hate Halloween—a fact you've known since forever. Do you remember me ever having a decent time at Halloween in this town?"

"What about the prank wars between the shifter and witches? I want to win!" said Tizzy.

"Ugh. That's the Halloween tradition I hate the most."

Prank wars sucked. The pranks were fairly harmless in the sense that no one was allowed to use supernatural abilities to pull off a prank. It was mostly things like rubber snakes in public toilets, turning the high school football field's uprights upside down, and using soap to write all over cars, sometimes, they could get very elaborate. My senior year, a few shifters had entombed our crotchety school librarian's car, a VW Beetle, inside the cafeteria's walk-in refrigerator. Ms. Fredrickson still works at the high school. She's a witch, so she hasn't aged much at all, but she'd never had much in the way of magical power, so the shifters hadn't had their furry asses zapped by her. But there had been a lot of detention handed out.

I shook my head at the soulful expression on my familiar's face. "No."

Tizzy skittered up my arm and flicked my ear to get my attention. "This could be a great way for the town to get to know the new sheriff."

"Chief of Police," I corrected, but only because the

Grand Inquisitor Clementine Battles aka my grand-mother had insisted I take the job. I owed her two favors and staying in Paradise Falls and taking the job had been favor number one. I didn't even want to think about what I would have to do for favor number two. She had showed up in Paradise Falls twice since we'd fought a rogue witch who'd joined with some shifters to pull off some horrific druidic magic that included killing my best friend's brother and almost killing my friend as well. I was more grateful than I could say for her help, but I still harbored some major resentment for her part in jailing my dad. Her son. Ugh. Sure, everyone thought he'd murdered my mother, and no one could predict it was an unbinding spell gone wrong. However, Clementine was his mother. She should have protected him.

I shook my head. Maybe I'd lived out in the human world for too long. Maybe expecting a witch, especially an old one, to choose her child over her duty was too much to ask. If it came down to it, would my father choose me?

"I am the chief of police," I said again mostly because it still sounded so weird to say it out loud.

The squirrel ignored me, obviously encouraged by this new line of thinking. "You know, it could be a total

4

public relations event. All the little furbabies and witchlets and their parents—"

I shook my hands at her in a mock-scary wave. "Having the crap frightened out of them by a flying squirrel?" I took another sip of coffee, sweet with just the right amount of French vanilla creamer, but it had already started to cool down. "You realize the whole town is full of very real and very scary monsters, right? A bowl of noodles and peeled grapes isn't likely to impress anyone." We really had been gone from town too long if Tizzy thought anything about Halloween in Paradise Falls might resemble a human celebration.

"We could do a demon theme with splashes of blood all over the wall, some black light highlighting ghostly handprints, and shrieking sound effects coming from the basement as if the bowels of hell have opened up to let all the demons out."

"That's not happening," a deep voice interrupted. "I like the color of my walls." Ford walked into the kitchen wearing tight jeans and a sky blue tight t-shirt. Whew, damn, he made my libido zing.

"Our walls," I reminded my grumpy but undeniably sexy mate. "Good morning, Ford."

As I glanced at my mate, all six-foot-nine-inches of

him, I stifled a girlish giggle. I found out several months earlier that we were true mates, like shifter mates, even though I'm a witch. With Shifters, it's a scent thing. To me, he smells like spicy desserts, and to him, I smelled like vanilla and rum.

It's a long story that involves a sloppy, drunken kiss our senior year. How was I to know my bold drunken move would imprint me on him? I was seventeen, for the love of red velvet cake. But looking at him now, I regretted nothing.

Except not spending the last seventeen years in his arms.

He was broad shouldered, and his light blue eyes were bright in contrast to his chocolate-colored hair. It had grown out a couple of inches into a mop of thick curls. Just the way I liked it. There was nothing like grabbing a handful of his soft silky mane while hollering his na —Uhm, you get my point. He had, however, shaved his short beard. Twice I'd gotten teased at the police station about the rug rash on my face, and that was enough to make me insist on him taking a razor to his scruff twice a day.

He kissed my cheek, and hot damn, the aroma of hot cinnamon rolls filled the air. I happily inhaled his scent as he poured himself a cup of coffee and sat down next to me at the center island. "Tizzy, we've been over this," he said.

Tiz balled her fingers into fists and put them on her hips. She gave me a pointed look. "Why does the bear get a say in this?"

"Because it's the bear's house," Ford said.

"Our house," I corrected, not admitting that his little slips of sole possession hurt my feelings.

"Our house," he amended.

I took a sip of my coffee. "Damn, it's cold already."

"Hello," Tizzy said. She pointed at me and wiggled her finger. "You should use your magic. It'll be good practice."

"Why would I do that when I can just pop the mug into the microwave. Easy peasy."

Ford looked up from his newspaper. "Didn't you promise the council president you'd practice?"

The council president was my father, and yes, I had promised him I would work on my craft. I huffed a sigh. "Fine." I stared down at the offending cup of cold coffee and worked up a sufficient spell to cast before weaving the words that would make my witch's brew boil.

"Caffeine, caffeine, strong and bright.

You keep me going from morn 'til night.

I like you black, I like you sweet.

You're no good cold, so bring the heat.

Done is done, Goddess grant to me.

Steaming hot java, so mote it be."

Tizzy, Ford, and I leaned forward as the dark liquid began to boil.

"I think it's working, Haze," Tiz said excitedly.

I leaned back as rapidly churning bubbles began to form in the dark liquid. "Huh. I'm not sure that's right." Suddenly, the coffee began to hiss.

"Should it be fizzing?" Ford asked.

"That's not good," I stated as steam arose like a thick fog above the cup.

"Oh, my Goddess!" Tizzy shouted as Ford and I stood up, and the stools we'd been sitting on clattered to the stone tile floor.

"Get away from ground zero," I ordered Tiz.

She jumped from the center island to the sink counter in a blazing quick leap while Ford and I stumbled back.

"It's going to blow!" Ford said.

We shielded our eyes against the impending disaster, all of us holding our breath while we waited for shattered pieces of the mug to go flying.

Nothing happened.

After a few seconds, I got brave enough to move back in for a second look. "Uh oh."

"What?" Ford asked. "What happened?"

I picked up the mug and tipped it sideways. The bottom was completely gone. Melted. There was a hole in the center island granite where the molten lava coffee had burned straight through. I opened the cabinet underneath. Tizzy scurried around my legs and peeked inside.

"Goddess, Haze. I hope that stuff doesn't burn a hole to China."

"It'll cool down before then." I hoped. "Or evaporate."

"It's magic," Tiz said. "It might not."

"Maybe we don't practice magic in the house, anymore," Ford suggested.

I wanted to remind him that he was the one who poked me to do it in the first stupid place, but I settled for sticking my tongue out at him. "Good idea."

He strolled over to me, his hulking body dwarfing me as he gathered me in his arms. He cupped the back of my neck, stealing my breath, as he kissed me deeply and soundly.

I growled my pleasure, which earned me a decent bottom squeeze. Ford smiled at my dazed expression. "Now isn't that a much better use of your tongue?"

"Ha ha." I tried to keep my knees from buckling beneath me. I stroked my fingertips across the short hair on the back of his neck and leaned forward to press my boobs against his muscular chest. "Keep this up, Ford Baylor, and you're going to be late for work."

He grinned and winked at me. "That's okay. I sleep with the boss."

Tizzy jumped up on the center island again. "Ugh. I can't watch you two do the bear-witch boogie. It's too early in the morning. I'm going to Lily's."

Lily Mason, my childhood best friend and the reason I was back in Paradise Falls, lived on the other side of town. Reluctantly, I slipped out of my mate's arms. "I'll drive you. I want to check in on Lily anyway." The reason I'd returned to Paradise Falls was to help Lily solve the mystery of her brother's death. She'd gotten the closure she deserved, but Danny had been the last of her family. I felt a keen responsibility to make sure she knew she wasn't alone.

I kissed Ford's cheek. "See you at the station."

He gestured to the center island. "Don't you think you should do something about the acid bath of coffee burrowing its way through the earth's core?"

I looked at Tiz. "It should be…okay, right?"

She shrugged. "I'll support whatever lie you want to tell yourself."

"It's not a big deal." I bit my lower lip then let it go. "I'll ask my dad about it when I get a free minute. Until then, maybe we could use some of that super foam to plug the hole in the floor."

The lights in the kitchen flickered then went out.

"I think it just took out the electrical wiring, Haze," Ford said.

"Fine!" I threw up my hands. "I'll call Dad now."

Ford grabbed his truck keys. "And I'll take Tizzy to Lily's."

"Only if I get to pick the music," Tizzy said.

My bear man shook his head. "Nope."

"I will jump out the window if I have to listen to country or western," she whined.

Ford waved at her. "It was nice knowing you."

"Behave. Both of you," I called after them.

Tizzy followed Ford down the hallway to the front door, while giving a rapid dissertation on country music and the downfall of society.

Goddess, I loved that squirrel.

CHAPTER 2

Daylight streamed in through the windows, so the kitchen wasn't completely devoid of light, but the freezer and the refrigerator didn't run on solar power. I stared at my phone on the counter, having a mental debate about whether I should call my father or not. I mean, did I really need him? How long could the coffee stay active-volcano hot, for Goddess sake?

"What I really needed was an electrician," I mumbled. I hadn't needed my father since I was seventeen-years-old. Did I really need him now?

A long, gurgling sound followed by a *clank, clank, clank* sounded as some major sparks flew from the ends of the exposed wires.

I grabbed my phone and punched my dad's name with

my index finger. The phone rang once before he answered.

He sounded worried. "Hazel? Is something wrong?"

I chewed off the corner of my fingernail then said, "Why would anything be wrong?"

"You only call me when something is wrong."

"That's so not fair." True, I thought, but definitely not fair.

His voice was suspicious. "So, nothing's wrong?"

I paused and weighed the merits of telling Dad about my sloppy witchery versus letting the coffee burn the toes of Chinese citizens on the opposite side of the world. I decided it was better to swallow my pride. "I think I turned my coffee into a Chernobyl incident."

"Huh?"

"We are having a serious meltdown here, and I need your help."

"Hah! I knew it."

"...."

"Hazel?"

"...."

"I'm on my way."

Since I was alone, I allowed myself a smug smile. "Thank you, Dad." I hung up.

The wires popped and crackled, scaring the smug right out of me. Dang it. My dad was an ace warlock. My mother had been a really powerful, albeit evil, witch, so why the heck couldn't I do something as simple as boil water? It shouldn't be this hard.

And yet, it always was.

I was nearly startled out of my standard issue, non-slip police loafers when my dad apparated next to me in the kitchen. "Okay, what happened?"

"Sweet baby Goddess! Are you trying to give me a heart attack?"

He wore a dark suit, his dark brown hair slick and neat. He tugged on a cuff. "It sounded urgent, and the fastest way here is a translocation spell."

I wrinkled my nose at him. "Next time translocate outside the front door and knock." Dad and I had finally gotten to a place where I didn't hate his face, but I wasn't ready to have him act like everything was fine. "This is my place, and you're a guest."

"I thought this was Ford's place?"

Ouch. He sure knew how to poke at my insecurities. "I live here. That makes it our place."

Dad shrugged and looked around. "Why are all the lights off?"

I glared at him. "I forgot to pay the bill."

My father's exasperated sigh was followed by the incantation, *"Light, light, make it bright."*

Instantly, the room was bathed in warm sunshine.

I pursed my lips, trying to hide how impressed I was by my dad's spell. If I had tried the same magic, it probably wouldn't have worked at all. Or I would have blinded the entire town.

He raised a brow. "Why is there a hole in your center island?"

"My coffee is eating its way to the earth's core right now." I held up the cup with the melted bottom. "Apparently."

My dad's eyes widened. "What did you do, Hazel?"

"This is your fault."

He tucked his chin, his expression incredulous. "How is it my fault?"

I crossed my arms. "You made me promise I would practice magic."

"I didn't tell you to do this."

All I wanted was a hot cup of coffee. Is that too much to ask?"

"Is your microwave broken?"

My lower lip extended out.

"Don't pout." He tapped my bottom lip, and I reeled it in. "Break it down for me."

"I cast a spell to heat my coffee. It went nuclear and burned a hole straight down through the cup, the center island, and the floor. Then the lights went out."

He nodded. "Did you specify the level of heat?"

"You're supposed to do that?"

"You should always be specific."

"You weren't specific when you lit up the kitchen. You just said to make it bright. How come we aren't living on the sun right now?"

"I am always specific, if not in word then in thought. This is what happens when you don't practice magic for almost two decades."

"Well, if I'd had parents interested in my education, maybe I wouldn't have turned out to be such a disaster."

He frowned. Hah! My dad wasn't the only one who could poke at insecurities.

"All that is behind us now."

"Is it really."

He crossed his arms, mirroring my stance. "It's time to move forward."

"I will if you will." I turned my finger in the air. "Now, how do I fix this?"

"Tell me what you said but leave out the intention behind the words unless you want another mishap."

"It's dumb."

"Just do it."

"Fine." I rolled my eyes. "Caffeine, caffeine, strong and bright. You keep me going from morn 'til night. I like you black, I like you sweet. You're no good cold, so bring the heat. Done is done, Goddess grant to me. Steaming hot java, so mote it be."

"What's with the 'so mote it be'? It's very archaic."

"I saw it in a Spells for Dumbasses book." I met his judgmental gaze. "It works."

Dad looked at the hole. "So well." He shook his head. "The spell is good. I think the problem lies in your execution."

"I just wanted it hot."

He snorted. "You got that and then some."

"Dad."

He held up a hand. "We need to reverse the spell."

"I'm afraid I'll turn my kitchen into the North Pole."

"Wrong holiday." He put his arm around my shoulder, and I fought against the impulse to stiffen and pull away. "Just remember that it's all in the intention behind the words. Make sure you have a clear idea of what you want to happen when you say the incantation."

"Okay, but if I start a blizzard, you better be ready to shut it down."

He nodded.

It took me a second to find the right words, but finally, I had them. I closed my eyes to concentrate.

"Coffee burning through my floor.

Cool down and flow no more.

I like you black, I like you sweet.

You're no good cold, but this is too much heat.

Reverse the spell, Goddess grant to me.

Tepid cup of joe, so mote it be."

I opened one eye. No explosions of snow. So far, so good. I opened the other eye and peered at my dad. "Did it work?"

He held his hand over the hole. "I don't feel any active magic." He smiled. "I think it worked. Good job, Hazel."

My emotions ran the gambit between elation and pride. "Thanks. And thanks for your help."

"I'm glad you felt like you could call me."

My cell phone rang, giving me the perfect excuse not to respond. The screen showed the police station number. "It's work. I have to take it."

He nodded. "Of course."

I answered the call. "Hello. Chief Kinsey here."

Officer Tamara Givens, typically a calm woman,

sounded breathy and frantic. "Chief, you need to get to Main and Bliss Street right away."

"What's happened?"

"By all reports, the mouth of hell just opened up smack dab in the center of town."

I looked at my dad, my eyes wide. "I'm on my way."

CHAPTER 3

The intersection of Main and Bliss bubbled as steam rippled off the oily black surface of a giant hissing puddle, reminding me way too much of my coffee misstep. Only this boiling yuck took up the entire center of the four-way. The strong aroma of over-done hardboiled eggs and burnt petroleum turned my stomach.

As I passed the crowd, I overheard angry Shifters damning the stinky abomination as a witch prank gone bad. Things like, "Damn witches." "Cheating." "No magic. No points." "Sore losers."

I put my hands in my jacket pockets as I strolled to Ford side. I took in the monstrous sight.

He shook his head. "I have no words."

"I think the crowd has plenty." I craned my head. "What in the world is this thing?"

"Your guess is as good as mine. It has to be magic. Right?"

"I'm the wrong witch to ask." I gestured to two of my deputies. "Get those bystanders back." I looked at Ford. "Why is Matty Deerfield's truck in the pit?"

A red pickup truck with rusted out back wheel wells had driven into the spontaneously formed tar pit, and the ass end was three feet off the ground as the front sank slowly into the boiling pitch. Matty, a stocky man who was my height, about five-eight with short reddish-brown hair, stood off to the side of the road, his arms crossed tightly over his broad chest and his face red with blustery anger.

"That's one pissed off weremole," Ford said. "It took three of us to pull him out of the vehicle and away from it," he waved his hands at the black pool in front of us, "whatever the hell that is. I had to threaten to arrest him if he didn't stay back from the scene."

"What charges?"

"Obstruction of law enforcement in the discharge of their duty." He glowered at the seething mole. "And for being a general pain in the ass."

"Is that against the law?" I chuckled. "Because I think Tizzy should be thrown into the clink."

He flashed a smile, and I felt my stomach flutter. My mate had some nice lip action.

"The natives are restless." I indicated the crowd. "Do you think witches are responsible for this?"

"It wasn't my people."

I raised a brow. "I thought I was your people."

"You know what I mean. During the week before All Hallows Eve, it's shifters versus witches. It's the way it's always been."

"Is the prank competition really so important?"

Ford stared at me. "Yes." Gosh, he looked so serious.

"Did something happen that you're not telling me about?"

He shuddered. "I don't want to talk about it."

I huffed a breath. "Gah! I hate Halloween." I scanned the crowd for guilty expressions. In my work as a field agent for the FBI, I had found that sometimes criminals liked to admire their handiwork, especially if it was something elaborate. You know, like putting a putrid pool of muck in the middle of a busy intersection. I recognized several people: the Shifters on the scene were Johnny Richards, a used car dealer, Matty Deerfield, of course, since it was his truck in the black bog, Mike Dandridge, a cougar shifter and the owner Dandridge Family Grocery, along with a few teenagers, Joanna Crandell, Tommy Lowe, and Lincoln Baylor, Ford's younger brother. Joanna, Tommy, and Lincoln all had parents on the Shifter-Witch Council. "I didn't realize your brother hung out with Joanna and Tommy."

He looked up at his brother with barely any interest and shrugged. "I guess so."

For the witches, Becksy Ansel, also a teenager and a waitress at Lolo's Diner, stood near Lincoln and the other teens. She worried her lower lip between her teeth. Lena Ansel, her mother, looked just as concerned. Romy Quinn, who I knew from when I was in high school, a *not-friend-but-not-enemy*, hugged her *totally-my-enemy* cat familiar to her chest.

Romy's familiar was a pearl-gray large Persia, and I hated the smart-mouthed ball of fluff with every inch of my being. She'd made my life hell during my formidable years. Romy was the only reason I hadn't tried to zap her out of existence. Well, Romy and my lack of any real spelling skills. She owned Modesta's Tea Haus over on Heavenly near the DMV, and I'd eaten there a couple of times since my return to town.

Romy made a great turkey, pesto, and cream cheese sandwich on artisan bread that was soft, delicious, and nutty.

My stomach gurgled. Great. Now I was hungry. Oh, wait. Nope. The gurgling was coming from the supernatural cesspit. Gross.

I skimmed the crowd again. I didn't see anyone who looked pleased by what was happening to the street. A prankster would have taken some glee in this kind of giant fiasco, right? "I don't think this is as simple as an attempt to win a competition."

"You really have been gone a long time if you think that."

A big bubble right rose from the black tar and popped, releasing more odious gas in my vicinity. "Yuck! What in the name of the Goddess is this crap?"

Ford looked at me then back at the roiling mess. "Your guess is as good as mine."

"What are the chances this is a natural event?" Maybe disgusting sludge pools spontaneously erupted around here, and I wouldn't have to chalk this up to the prank wars or to Halloween nonsense, or worse, an attack on our town.

Ford gave me side-eye. "No chance."

"Damn it."

He shrugged, this hint of a smile tugging at the corner of his lips. "Maybe your attempt to heat coffee this morning had bigger side effects than burning through the kitchen floor."

I looked around at all the amazed, irritated, and scared expressions in the crowds forming at each of the crossings. I snapped my gaze up at my very tall and suddenly very amused boyfriend. "You can just keep that theory to yourself, mister. I don't need all the witch haters turning their furry rage on me."

But what if he was right? My magic was unpredictable. My grandmother had hinted that my powers were stronger than I believed, what if I had inadvertently tampered with the forces of nature in an effort to enjoy my morning beverage? Goddess, I hoped like heck I wasn't the source of this chaos. I didn't even want to think about what my grandmother would have to say on the subject. I am ninety-nine percent sure that the promise my father extracted from me to practice magic had been at her behest.

The *clack-clack* of heels on the sidewalk behind me made me grit my teeth. I'd spent enough time over the past several months getting to know that strident gate well. I turned around as I plastered on a fake smile and fought back a groan as a tall, leggy, red-head approached. "Tanya," I said. "What are you doing here?"

Tanya Gellar, the town's current medical examiner and doctor, placed an elegant hand on her pencil-skirted hip. "Well, hello to you, too."

Ford nudged me. "Be nice," he muttered.

I frowned at him. At one point, Tanya had set her sights on Ford. Luckily, he only had eyes, well, the mating scent, anyhow, for me. "I haven't set her hair on fire," I muttered back. "That's pretty nice if you ask me."

She and I had replaced the recently deceased Adele Adams and Dirk Nichols to represent the witches on the Shifter Coalition board, and our relationship could be best described as contentious. In other words, we didn't like each other. I liked the way she looked at my mate even less.

Tanya thrust her boobs forward—I might be projecting here—as she looked at the town's new tourist attraction. "Chief, how come I had to get this call from a civilian?"

"As far as I know, there isn't a dead body around her for you to examine." I scanned the crowd again, this time for Tanya's source. "Who called you?" I wanted to make sure I struck them off my Christmas card list.

"That's none of your business." She actually blushed, which made me want to know who the tattletale was even more.

"I just got here. I haven't had time to assess the scene, let alone make any phone calls to people necessary to the scene." I emphasized necessary, because she did not fall into that category.

Tanya looked down her thin, perfect nose at me. "You're so petty. That's not a good look on you." She peered at the black lack of goo and made a face. "Ewww. It stinks," she said.

"Is that your professional opinion?" I asked, ignoring the fact that it had been my first observation as well. I stepped closer to get a better look at the burbling pool.

Ford put his hand on my shoulder. "Don't get too close, babe."

"That's Chief Babe to you," I said.

"What in the nine unholy hells?" The booming voice belonged to my sort of father-in-law, and yet another council member, Bryant Baylor.

My father, who had suddenly appeared, said, "This is definitely rooted in magic."

My face felt tight. "You think? It doesn't take Albus Dumbledore to recognize that the gooey lake in the middle of the intersection isn't a natural occurrence." The idea that I might have somehow caused this made my heart turn over in my chest. *Goddess, don't let this be my fault.*

Ford cast a questioning glance my way, so I answered with a glare that I hoped would keep his mouth zipped.

Bryant addressed my dad. "Pranks using magic are forbidden," he said as he waved a meaty hand. "No points for the witches."

I rolled my eyes. The rules had been the big debate at the last coalition meeting. During the prank wars, points were awarded based on three things: finesse, creativity, and awe factor. This tar pit definitely pushed the limits of all three categories. No magic or Shifter abilities could be used to perpetrate a prank. Keeping the pranks mundane put the witches and Shifters on a level playing field.

When the prank competition came up, Ford told me, and with more pride than I thought necessary, that the Shifters had taken home the prank prize, a crystal bear paw holding a wand, for the past twelve years in a row. Something the witches, especially the younger ones, were not too happy about.

A brown and white cat rubbed against Tanya's leg. She

lifted the fluffy animal into her arms. "What do you think, Jup?"

"I've never seen anything like this before," the cat said. His brow furrowed, and his whiskers twitched.

Tanya scratched him between the ears. "I was afraid you'd say that." She gave me a grim look. "Jupiter has the ability to remember all his past incarnations as a familiar. He once belonged to a powerful witch who was killed during the Salem Witch Trials."

Of course, her familiar's name was Jupiter, the king of Roman gods. Since he'd offered nothing helpful to the situation, I was understandably less impressed than she was by his observation. Frankly, it bugged me that Tanya was so high and mighty about her familiar. So, inexplicably, I blurted, "Tizzy was once the familiar of Cleopatra."

"Cleopatra wasn't a witch," Jupiter said.

"So, you're an expert on Egyptian witches too?"

The bratty tabby stuck his tongue out at me. I'd have to catch Tizzy up to speed later. I was sure that familiar gossip got around as quickly as the witch news.

Bryant Baylor crossed his arms over his massive chest. "What are you going to do about this, Chief?"

I glanced at Ford. "Call Steve Crandell." Steve was the

new *paullulum mammalia* aka tiny critters alpha. His predecessor, Robert Townsend, had been one of the people responsible for my friend Lily's grief. I had never been so glad to watch someone get dismembered.

Yeah, you heard me right. My beau tore that bastard limb from limb. And while having Ford covered in blood had been unappealing, washing the gunk of our enemies off his super studly body had been very rewarding.

Steve had been the natural replacement to lead the small critters, but that wasn't why I wanted him called. He owned Crandell Quarries, and his company had the road maintenance contract for the town streets. "Ask him to bring concrete barriers and some gravel here. We'll try to fill in the pit, and if that doesn't work, we'll block it off. If we can't resolve this quickly, we may have to call in the big guns."

Tanya groaned. "Don't call the Grand Inquisitor. Not yet."

On this, we both agreed. "Last resort," I said.

Two of my patrol officers, John Parker and Mitzy Thomas, used orange and white traffic tape to resurrect a barricade around the hazard. I gave Mitzy, a tall, brunette wolf Shifter, a nod of approval. Her partner, a tow-headed warlock, to pretty to be handsome, kept his head down as they diligently worked in tandem to attach the tape to the four stop signs. Their partnership was typical for the Paradise Falls Police Department. Pairing witches and Shifters cut down on discrimination complaints. The whole town, on the surface, appeared to be the epitome of equality.

"Do you think a witch is a responsible for this?" Bryant asked. "Is it a prank gone wrong?"

"Or something worse," Ford added.

Before I could ponder the "something worse," a woman shouted, "Help!" Her voice pierced the crowd's chatter. "Help me!"

CHAPTER 4

E veryone in the area froze for a moment before
we all turned toward the sound emanating from
one of three businesses. UnBearably Beautiful Salon,
owned by Marlene Edwards, a bear shifter. Pierce
Roberts, CPA. Pierce was a warlock, and a wizard with
numbers. I'd been thinking about hiring him to do my
taxes. The third business on that side of Main Street
was the Blissful Bakery, owned by Milo and Jenny
Weaver. Jenny's desserts were better than a Xanax. I
suspected magic was one of her staple ingredients, but
since no one ever complained, I didn't interfere. Hell,
I'd sampled her goods once or twice on a bad day.

Jenny came running out from between her shop and
Robert's office. She was waving her arms frantically.
"Over here! There's a body."

My stomach dropped. I glanced at Ford, his mouth set in a grim line. The tar pit suddenly seemed less interesting to the crowd as well.

"Parker! Thomas!" I yelled to my officers. "Keep civilians back."

I didn't wait for their acknowledgment. I motioned Tanya to join Ford and me as we briskly crossed the street. Jenny Weaver's neck and cheeks were red. A faint sheen of sweat had broken out on her brow. When we reached her, she heaved a loud sob.

She clutched her chest. "I...I...I was just..."

"Take a deep breath," Ford said, his deep voice soothing. "There, there," he added as she did as he instructed. "Now, tell us about the body."

"It's," she hiccupped, "around back. In the dump. I was," she hiccupped again, "taking out the trash when I saw it."

"What did you see?" I asked.

"Two legs sticking out from under the lid." She choked back a sob and hiccupped at the same time, forcing a fart that made the air around her butt sparkle.

Ford's eyes widened.

"Oh Goddess," Tanya whispered.

"I'm sorry," Jenny cried. "That happens when I'm upset."

"Take us to the body," I said.

She sniffled and nodded, then led us between the buildings to the back of the bakery. A large blue trash bin was seated just outside Blissful's backdoor. And just like Jenny had said, two legs were sticking out from under the lid. The victim wore close-toed gold and green pumps with three-inch block heels and a pair of dark green slacks.

Tanya put her hand over her mouth to stifle a gasp.

"What?" I asked.

"I recognize those shoes," she said. "They belong to Agatha Milan."

"The witch who lives out on the south side of town?"

Tanya nodded solemnly. "She owns Milan Fashion just up the street." She clutched her orange and black leather purse decorated with gold grommets out to me. "She designed this bag for me."

I had to admit it was a nice-looking purse. "Let's not jump to any conclusions until we see more than shoes."

If it wasn't Agatha, I would check out her store when I had a free minute.

Ford took pictures of the area with his phone. After, he put on a pair of gloves and lifted the bin lid. The legs, now unevenly weighted, flopped out onto the ground.

Tanya yipped. Jenny fainted. I'll admit, I was stunned.

There was no body attached to the appendages.

Ford knelt for a closer look. He lifted up a pant leg. "Rubber." He looked up at me. "Or silicone."

"So not real."

He shook his head. "If I had to guess, I'd say, prank."

Tanya tended to Jenny, who moaned as she came around.

"Who would go through the trouble to cast fake legs in rubber?"

"Or someone ordered them online," Ford said.

We didn't get deliveries here in Paradise Falls, but we had our version of a postal clerk, Will Bently, who picked up packages in the next town over. Still, online shopping was discouraged because Will's van wasn't built for volume.

"We should ask Will about recent recipients of anything bigger than a bread box." I sigh, thankful there wasn't a homicide to investigate on top of everything else going on. "Halloween sucks."

"There's a big S carved in the calf," Ford said. He smiled. "Points to the Shifters."

Apparently, I was alone in my dislike of the current fall festivities.

"Wait," said Tanya. "The Shifters stole a witch's shoes and pants for this childish prank?"

"Don't hate," said Ford. "It's not against the rules."

Tanya opened her mouth, but I held up a hand. "Enough." I turned to Ford. "Someone had to see something."

"We aren't seriously going to investigate this," he said.

"Don't be silly. This has been enough of a distraction from the bigger problem at hand. Take statements from the business owners around here and start evacuating the area. If the gloopy pond in the street starts growing, it could swallow everything around here."

Ford's lips thinned in a dour expression. "I'll take Marlene Edwards' beauty shop. She and my mom are friends."

"Good idea. I'll take Robert Pierce, the accountant." Paradise Falls Theater, a historic landmark in town, was across the street from UnBearably Beautiful. The marquee advertised a double feature of *Night of the Living Dead* and *Dawn of the Dead*. On the opposite side of the road were a few fashion boutiques, a sporting goods shop, and a pawnshop. I gestured toward them. "I'll take one side of the street, you take the other. We can work our way to the corners at the intersection."

"Sounds like a plan," Ford said. He kissed my cheek. "See you on the other side, Chief Babe."

ROBERT PIERCE, A THIN MAN WITH SANDY BLOND HAIR and deep-set green eyes, sat in a high-back leather chair at a large, cherry wood desk, typing away at a computer. His small office was painted a pale blue with forest green accents. Plants lined the front windows, giving his place of business a comfortable warmth.

He looked up at me when I walked in, his mouth skewed in an annoyed pucker. "Can I help you?"

I flashed him my badge. "I'm Special...err...Police Chief Hazel Kinsey." I'd spent so many years as Special Agent Kinsey, I was still trying to adjust to the new title.

"I know who you are," Pierce said, turning his attention back to his keyboard. "You're the one who murdered Adele."

Adele Adams had been an utterly rotten egg, but that didn't mean she hadn't had friends in the community. You don't live for two hundred years without forming allies. I didn't rise to his bait. "If that's how you want to see it, I'm okay with that."

He stopped typing and glared at me. "What do you want?"

I was tempted to arrest him for acting like a Class A Asshole. "When did you come into work this morning?"

"Are you interrogating me?"

"If you haven't noticed, someone or something has turned your street into a big, boiling cauldron of awful."

For the first time since I'd walked in, I saw something other than irritation in his eyes. He appeared genuinely surprised. "What are you talking about?"

"How far up that computer's ass has your head been all day?" I pointed out the window and down the street. "At the intersection."

He stood up and walked, his gait rigid and stiff, to the

window. He frowned as he stared, wide-eyed, at the mess. "Like a hellbroth boil and bubble," he whispered, pretentiously quoting Shakespeare.

"Double, double, toil and trouble," I said. Two could play the Macbeth game.

He gave me a contemptuous glare. "That wasn't there when I came in this morning."

"You sure?"

"I think I would have noticed, Special Police Chief Kinsey."

If this guy didn't stop acting like a jerk, I was going to shoot him. "You haven't seen anything suspicious since your arrival? Anyone strange passing your front windows?"

"People pass by here all the time. It's a busy street."

We were both looking to the right toward the oil pit when a loud bang on the window startled us back. A clown pressed its body against the glass and rubbed a big red kiss on the pristinely clean glass. After, it honked a horn and ran across the street and down an alley. *Oh, great more Halloween pranks.* Clowns? Really? "

"Goddessdamn Shifters!" Pierce shouted as he shook a

fist. He looked young, but he reminded me of the old human men complaining about kids these days.

"You need to evacuate your office, Mr. Pierce. We don't know if that thing will get bigger." I smiled at him sweetly. "It would just devastate me if the pond of sticky grossness swallowed you up."

"I'm sure it would." He shook his head. "I have too much work to do, so I'm staying." He held up a hand. "I'll keep an eye out. If it gets worse, I'll go."

Why, oh, why did people always try to weather the storm? "I'm afraid this isn't a request, sir."

"Are you going to kill me if I don't listen to you? Is that what happened with Adele?"

"Adele was murdering Shifters, and she tried to kill me," I snapped. Ugh. Why was I letting this jerkface get to me?

He sniffed and lifted his chin. "I've heard the propaganda, but I'm not some gullible towny you can manipulate with lies."

Fantastic. A conspiracy nut. "Whatever, Oliver Stone. Just get your crap and get the hell out of this area before I arrest you for your own safety."

"Fine," he huffed. "But this is how tyranny starts."

I wagged my finger at him. "When I come back this way, you best be gone, buddy." I pushed my way past Pierce and exited his office. Out on the sidewalk, Ford was talking to a very tall woman, well over six feet.

When I reached him, he said, "Haze, this is Marlene Edwards. Marlene, meet Police Chief Haze Kinsey."

"So, you're the woman who landed our Ford." She smiled at him fondly then at me. "You come in anytime for a haircut, Haze." She gave my blonde hair an appraising look. "It's cute, but it can use a little trim. First one is on the house." Marlene gave off a warm and inviting vibe.

"Thanks. I'll take you up on that."

Ford put his hand on my shoulder. "Marlene says she hasn't seen anything unusual this morning. But she did see when the tarry stuff appeared."

"I was outside getting some air, and all of a sudden there was a groaning noise, and *poof*, there it was." She put her hand to her chest. "That poor Matty Deerfield, his business has been struggling this year and losing his only truck is going to hurt badly."

I gave a sympathetic nod. "Did you see anyone else outside at the time?"

"No one strange. Jenny Weaver had just crossed the street and went into her muffin shop."

I glanced up the street toward the bakery. "Coming from where?"

Marlene shook her head. "Oh, I don't know. Maybe some of the shops down the way."

"Anyone else you recognized?" I asked. "The more people who might have witnessed the event, the more we might be able to piece together how it happened."

"Well, I saw Lincoln and some of his friends." She peered at Ford. "It's a school day, so I gave him a hard time about skipping."

Ford frowned. "I'm not his keeper." He didn't talk much about Lincoln. I assumed they weren't close because of the age difference, but maybe there was something there I didn't know about. "Who was he with?"

"Becksy Ansel, Joanna Crandell, and Tommy Lowe."

"What were they—"

A clown jumped out in front of us, honked a handheld horn, hurled a fist full of confetti at Ford, and then started doing a jig. His rainbow-colored hair shook with every movement, his grin painted to resemble a tooth-filled maw, and his eyes circled with black.

Ford screamed. Well, as close to a scream as a man with his low vocal range could muster. He staggered back, his eyes wide and his skin as pale as moonlight. If I didn't know any better, I'd think he was getting ready to keel over from shock.

The clown laughed, honked again, jumped between us, and bopped Ford on the head with a foam bat.

Ford pulled out his weapon and aimed at the clown's large red bow tie. "Die, you bastard!" he yelled.

The clown clutched his bat and took off across the street, disappearing around the corner as he headed down Angel's Grove Street.

Ford whirled, gun raised to shoot Bozo in the back, and I grabbed his arm. "Don't kill the clown!"

He stopped, straightened, and holstered his weapon. His eyes still looked wild as he scanned the area.

"Are you okay, honey?" Genuine concern wound through me. As I touched his shoulder, I could feel him shaking. What was wrong with him?

Bright tinkles of laughter gained our attention. I turned sharply toward the offender. Or, as I quickly observed, offenders. Plural. My best friend Lily was standing off to the side with a guffawing Tizzy on her shoulder. At least Lily had the good taste to keep her laughter to a quiet snicker. Tizzy, however, laughed so hard she lost her balance and fell off Lily's shoulder.

The squirrel recovered before she landed smoothly onto the sidewalk. "Sweet Goddess in a tutu," Tizzy said, wiping tears from her eyes. "Ford Baylor is afraid of clowns."

CHAPTER 5

I absconded the scene with Lily and Tizzy after I put Ford in charge of the patrol officers. I trusted him to handle the interviews and the evacuation. Besides, after the clown incident, he needed something to do, and I needed to make sure squirrel and werecougar weren't added to his lunch menu.

We went to Modesta's Tea Haus for lunch. Romy Quinn, the owner, had been in the crowd this morning, and I wanted to talk to her. Of course, my choosing to interview her had nothing to do with the Turkey Pesto sandwich on soft Artisan bread I held in my hand. I made an *mmmmm* sound as I chewed.

"Stop that," Tizzy said. "You sound like a gerbil." Her narrow shoulders shuddered.

"What the heck happened to the road, Haze?" Lily asked.

I felt a weird compulsion to answer her question, not that I knew anything relevant or secret. "Your guess is as good as mine." As soon as I said it, the compulsion dissipated. Wierd. I took another bite. "I…" *Mmmm-mmmm.* After some quick chews, I swallowed. "I'm guessing some witch got carried away with a prank." At least that seemed to be the consensus. "But I don't understand why. A magical prank doesn't help the witches win."

"Maybe they meant it to be something small, and they messed up the spell or something."

Tizzy shook her head. "Haze is the only one who could mess up magic that bad, and I would have felt it if she'd pulled off that kind of power."

I poked my fork at her. "Hey! I'm not that bad."

"You're worse," Tizzy said. "But buck up, buttercup." She placed one paw over her heart and the back of the other to her forehead and affected her best Scarlett O'Hara impression. "After all, tomorrow is another day."

"Frankly, my dear, I don't give a damn." I took another bite of the sandwich and hummed.

Lily put her elbows on the table to draw our attention and stop the fight. "So, it would take a lot of power to make a lake of boiling tar in the middle of town, right?"

"I suppose so." I looked to Tizzy for confirmation.

She shook her head. "Sometimes I'm ashamed to call you my witch."

I smirked. "Aww, don't be like that."

"You two," Lily said. She smiled, but it didn't reach her eyes. "It's nice. I'm so happy for you, Haze. You have Ford now. And," she smiled fondly at the squirrel, "Tizzy, of course."

My heart ached for my friend. Both her parents had been killed our senior year, and less than a year ago, her younger brother had been murdered. All part of Adele Adam's plan to rule the world by turning Shifter pain into powerful druidic magic. Robert Pierce could be as pissy as he wanted to be with me, but I don't regret stopping Adele. Not one bit.

"You doing okay, Lils?"

"Yeah." She sighed. "Danny always loved Halloween. The prank competition seemed to bring out the best in him. It was the one time a year I didn't feel like a complete failure as a surrogate parent."

Lily, at the young age of eighteen, had become her little brother's guardian. He'd been seven at the time. With Danny gone, she had no family left, at least none that I knew of. With the exception of Tiz and me, she felt alone in her community.

I put my non-sandwich holding hand over Lily's. "I'm sorry, babe. If it's any consolation, you can join me in my hatred for all things Samhain."

Mike Dandridge walked in with Matty Deerfield and sat at the table across from us. "I can't believe my truck is gone," Matty said.

"You have insurance, right?" Mike said.

Matty didn't answer.

"Hey, Mike," I said. "How's business?"

"The grocery business is good," he said. "No short supply of people who want to eat."

"Ain't that the truth?" Between the crazy metabolism of shifters and witches, I was surprised there was any food in the world left for anyone else. "How's Veronica and the kids?" Veronica was a receptionist at the police station. She'd been working there for twenty years now, and she had made me feel welcome from my first day on the job.

"Good," he said. "I'll tell Veronica you asked after her."

A honking drew our attention to the front windows. The clown from earlier, his big shoes flopping out in front of him, high stepped his way past the Tea Haus.

"Goddess," Lily said. "Crowns are so creepy." She looked at Mike, who hadn't stopped staring. "Don't you think so?" she asked him.

"No. I really like clowns." He stared at her. "Like, really like them." He looked down at his tenting pants and back up at Lily, his cheeks red with embarrassment. "Uhm, I have to go...er...help my guys...or something." He covered his groin with crossed hands as he fled from the place.

I inclined my head to Lily. "What in the world was that all about?" I asked quietly.

She made a face and shrugged. "That was more information than I ever wanted to know about Mike."

"You? His wife works for me. I'm going to be thinking about him and clowns now every time I see her now."

She giggled. "Well, he's definitely more interesting than I thought he was."

"You mean disturbed."

"Now, Hazel. I get the feeling he told us something he had no intention of telling. Maybe we could just pretend we didn't hear it."

"There's not enough ear bleach in the world," Matty said. "I think I'll go see if they were able to pull my truck out." He got up and walked out.

"Shifter hearing," I said, and I shook my fists with a half-hearted triumph. "Yay."

I'd taken my privacy outside of a supernatural community for granted, and it made me forget sometimes that there was no such thing as privacy when therianthropes were around. Speaking of lack of privacy, I couldn't believe Tiz hadn't weighed in on Dandridge and his clown-fetish.

That is until a gray Persian cat with olivine green eyes, whom Tizzy had been watching with complete enrapt attention, leaped up onto the table. "Hello, Tisiphone," she purred.

Tizzy squeaked in alarm. The cat rolled onto her side in front of Tizzy and stretched. "Long time, no see."

"Who's your friend, Tiz?" Lily asked.

"This is Lumpypits," I said. "Romy Quinn's familiar." I'd always gotten along with Romy, but her familiar was a mean, snarky ball of cute. The cuteness just made her nastiness even uglier.

"It's Lupitia, cretin," the cat said to me. To Tizzy, she added, "I can't believe you've stuck with this loser all these years. I'd have petitioned the familiar council for a new witch, if I were you. Yours is definitely broken."

"Well, I can't believe your witch puts up with such an unimaginative familiar. It must make her magic so very dull," I said.

Tizzy, too stunned to speak apparently, crammed a large Brazil nut into her mouth.

So much for having my back.

Lily's claws came out, and she tapped them in front of the cat and bared a little fang as she said, "Amscray kitty before I show you how the big cats play."

Lupitia's eyes bugged as she scrambled off the table. Tizzy ate another nut.

"I can't believe you didn't let her have it, Tiz. What's up?"

"Nuffin'," she muttered as she chewed.

A shriek silenced the entire restaurant. Romy Quinn ran out of the kitchen, her eyes wide with terror. I rushed past her, expecting a dead body or something equally as horrible. Instead, I slipped on the slick floor and was dropped right into the middle of the apocalypse. Flames enveloped the oil fryers as the greasy liquid boiled over the edges, the sink faucets gushed water out onto the floor, and a white powder covered the burners and walls. An explosion rang my ears. I scrambled backward, my feet slipping in the oily water.

My eyes burned as acrid smoke ate up the oxygen around me. I heard my name, but it sounded muffled after the explosion. A hand grabbed the back of my shirt and hauled me out to the dining room. I blinked through the tears that had formed because of the irritants and my vision cleared. Lily was yelling something at me. I am six inches taller than her and outweigh her by a good forty pounds, but she hauled me up like a professional strongman. I felt Tizzy's claws on my legs as she climbed up to my shoulder.

When I turned my head to look at her, all the while, Lily moving us toward the door, Tizzy grabbed my face. "Haze!" She tweaked my nose. "Are you all right? You don't seem all right. Lily, I think the explosion damaged her brain!"

My hearing was finally coming back, but I wasn't sure if that was a good thing or not. "We have to get everyone out of here," I said, my throat hoarse from smoke inhalation.

"We already did," Lily said as we walked to the curb. Sirens in the distance meant the fire department was on the way.

Romy clutching Lumpita to her chest, big fat tears rolling down her alabaster cheeks, ran up to me. "I don't understand," she said. "I...I..."

"Tell me what happened?" Luckily witches recover quickly from injuries, it's in our genetics, but I still felt a bit wheezy from inhaling grease smoke. "What started the fire?"

"I don't know," she sobbed. "I had just cast a clean-up spell, and the oil fryers began to smoke. The next thing I know, flames are rolling across the counters and spilling onto the floor. I tried to cast a water spell to put them out, but then the pipes and faucets started clanking and rattling." Her matted chestnut brown hair clung to her neck. "Then *blam!* Water started spraying everywhere. Since my spells seemed to make everything worse, I tried throwing flour and salt down, but nothing slowed the fire down."

"Do you think someone sabotaged your kitchen?"

She shook her head. "I don't know how they could."

I thought about my coffee incident, how a simple heating spell had gone radioactive in a heartbeat. "Has your magic been reliable?"

"Yes," she said. "Always."

"Romy knows her stuff, you walking disaster," Lupoopiehead added.

"Hey, don't talk to Hazel like that." Tizzy's tail tightened on my throat. "She almost died in there."

"Her ineptitude must be contagious," the cat said.

Tizzy's little body went rigid.

"Easy there, girl." I stroked her fur. The fire crew, a five-person operation that consisted of five witches with infinity for earth magic, stood in front of the burning business.

"Out, out fire and flame," they chanted in unison. Their auras turned red as the heaviness of the spell filled the air around me. They grew louder. *"Out, out fire and flame."* Their auras turned into a thick red miasma that flexed and retracted.

Lily's eyes widened. "Do you see that?"

The weight and power of the spell made my knees weak. "Is that normal?" I asked Tiz.

"Nope," she squeaked. "Run!"

Lily grabbed my hand and yanked me into a sprint moving away from the restaurant. We got about ten feet when the massive explosion threw us down on the sidewalk. Concrete debris and ash rained down on me as I struggled to catch my breath.

I felt for Tizzy. She was no longer on my neck. I swallowed a hard knot of fear as my pulse quickened. "Tiz?" I coughed, my chest aching with the effort. I was pretty sure I'd broken a couple of ribs. "Tizzy," I said louder.

I turned my head and saw her running toward me. She jumped off a piece of fallen brick and leaped into the air, her arms and legs spreading wide, in a display that said, "That's right, bitches, I'm not just a squirrel, I'm a fabulous, flying squirrel!"

"Magnificent," Lupitapocket's said. I looked at her, and she shrugged before sauntering off to her witch, her tail swishing like a cat who caught the mouse.

"Catch me, Haze!" Tiz shouted, and I snagged her from the air.

Ouch. Raising my arms had made my ribs hurt even worse. "What happened to you?"

"I wanted to make sure no one else was left inside," she said.

"Well, no hero shit from you, you hear me?" The brief second I'd thought she'd been caught in the explosion had filled me with such a heavy grief. I didn't know what my life would be without her, and I never wanted to find out.

"Me," she laughed. "A hero? Forget about it."

Tizzy glanced Romy's way, watching as the witch hugged her stupid cat. There was a wistful expression in my familiar's eyes. Did she wish I was more like Romy? Goddess, I hoped not. Maybe the furball had been right. Maybe Tizzy would have been better off trading up for a better witch.

"Are you okay, Tiz?"

She wiggled her nose. "If I'd had known you were taking us to a bonfire for lunch, I'd have brought marshmallows."

Lily put her hand on my arm. "I see Ford's truck."

"Oh, and look," Tizzy added. "The weenie has brought himself. Lily, did you bring the roasting sticks?"

I laughed. It hurt. Goddess help me, I loved my familiar.

CHAPTER 6

Ford's truck roared up the street and screeched to a halt outside the perimeter established by the patrol officers. Real firefighters, with water hoses and stuff, squirted down the area with water and foam. The fire had mostly extinguished in the blast. No oxygen meant no fuel for the flames. He almost fell out of the cab as he shoved the door open. He ran past the growing crowd and only slowed when he saw me.

He reached me in seconds, his fingers tucking my hair back behind my ears. I was certain he was trying to see if either one of them had been blown off in the explosion. Next, he moved his hands down my arms. "Hello," he said.

My skin tingled at his touch, and the warm smell of cinnamon rolls overtook the pungent scent of smoke and burnt oil. "Hi," I said, wanting more than anything to roll around in his yummy aroma. When he touched my ribs, I winced.

"Hurt?" His voice was raw. I could see the fur rippling just beneath his human skin. It was taking every ounce of my mate's willpower to hold it together.

I wanted to ease his anxiety with a good cuddle followed by a voracious boinking. "Just some bruised ribs," I told him.

"Cracked?"

"Maybe." I reached up and caressed his cheek. "I'm okay. I promise."

He nodded and kissed my forehead. "We're going to run out of crime scene tape if this keeps up."

I let him help me to my feet. "I'll add ordering more to my to-do list. Right now, I have to figure out why the town is turning into Armageddon."

"First, we need to have Tanya look at your sides," he insisted.

I did a little insisting of my own. "Nope. Not going to happen. I'd sooner suffer through a punctured lung."

"Haze," Ford cajoled. "Tanya is a good doctor."

"She can see me when I'm dead." As if summoned like an evil spawn of hell in a teen horror flick, Tanya and my father crossed the police tape into the destruction zone. "Speak of the devil. And why is my father with her?"

"Hazel," my dad said, his brow creased with worry. "Are you okay? You look terrible. Your hair is singed. Are you burned?" Annoyingly, he was checking me over.

"I'm fine, Dad." I rolled my eyes. "Really."

"I suspect she broke a few ribs," my traitorous mate said.

"I can fix that," Tanya said.

"No," my father said. "No magic."

Wait. I narrowed my gaze at him. "What's going on? What do you know?"

"I've been getting reports on magic going awry since early this morning. I even had an incident myself. I tried to transport myself back to the coalition after I saw you at the tar lake, and I ended up out by the quarries instead. When I tried again, I found myself knee deep at the edge of Eden lake." He shook his head. "I had my phone on me, so I called for a ride back into town, but witches and warlocks all over town are having control issues with their magic now. It's definitely getting worse."

"That must be why the restaurant blew up," I said. "We need to call a town meeting, but until we can get everyone together, we need to get a phone tree going to warn all the witches not to cast spells for now."

"They're not going to like that," Tanya said, her own distaste showing in her pinched expression.

"They'll enjoy burning the world down around their ears even less."

"Chief!" Mitzy Thomas shouted. This was a banner day for her and Parker. "There's someone under a piece of wall on the side of the building."

"Goddess, no," Romy Quinn said. "Please tell me I didn't kill someone."

I couldn't give her the answer she wanted, so I didn't respond. Instead, I moved into action. "Show me."

Ford and our entourage of Tizzy, Lily, Dad, and Tanya, followed my curvy patrol officer around the side of Modesto's. Two legs, clothed in burned embroidered flare leg jeans and wearing red and white saddle shoes with two-inch heels, protruded from the wall.

"I recognize the shoes and those pants," Tanya said. "Those belong to Agatha, too."

Again? Was someone stealing Agatha Milan's clothes to perpetuate another hoax? Tanya didn't seem as upset this time, and I understood why. I suspected the Shifters were pulling the same prank again. But why was Agatha Milan being targeted? "Did you touch or move anything, Thomas?" I asked my officer.

Parker stepped in and said, "We didn't want to move anything or contaminate the scene, Chief."

Mitzy's expression soured. She hadn't liked him answering for her, but she didn't say anything. I liked Mitzy Thomas, but she would have to get tougher if she wanted to work in law enforcement. Especially, if she wanted to work law enforcement in a paranormal town.

Tizzy climbed up on my shoulder. "Those jeans are retrolydelicious. Very cool."

"And could be connected to a dead body," I said dryly.

"Very sad," she added. "I like the shoes, too. Do you think they come in my size? Or even better, yours?"

"Tizzy."

"What? You could stand a new wardrobe update, Haze."

"Not in the middle of a crime scene." I booped her on the nose with my finger. "Decorum."

She gave my hair a gentle tug. "You hid me away from people for nearly two decades. It's no wonder I don't know how to behave in public."

"Uh huh." She knew exactly how to act to push all my buttons. If there happened to be a corpse this time, I didn't want Tiz or my BFF here. Lily had been through enough already. I turned to my best friend. "Lily, can you take Tizzy home?"

"Sure," she said. She held up her hands, and Tizzy, with a despondent sigh, climbed into her cupped palms.

"She such a party pooper," Tizzy said to Lily.

"We can go shopping on the way home," Lily replied. "A little retail therapy will perk you right up."

"Awesome. I'm almost out of walnuts at home!"

"Take her, take her," I said, shooing Lily and Tizzy from the scene.

Ford knelt by the protruding legs. He motioned Tanya over. "Do you want to check them?"

She'd already gloved up, probably when I'd been

arguing with my tricky rodent. She lifted the pant hem and pushed at the leg underneath with her fingertips. "Rubber or silicone again. This is not Agatha Milan. Just two fakes again with her clothes and shoes. She twisted the calf sideways and revealed a carved in S. "I think it's our same prankster."

"Or pranksters," I said. "Could be more than one."

"Do you think S stands for Shifters?" Parker asked.

"Ford seems to think so." And I had as well but targeting one witch seemed strange. "If it is, they will make a claim for the competition. It could be an initial, though, or even a symbol. Let's not jump to conclusions. Besides, artificial legs are a pain in the ass for us to have to investigate but there's no real harm. We really need to focus our attention on the less mundane problems happening in town."

Mitzy leveled a cold gaze at her partner. "I agree, Chief."

"I'm so glad," I said with more sarcasm than I meant. Ugh. Too many years of hanging out with a particular squirrel.

Parker smirked.

"Is there a problem here?" I asked.

"No, Chief," they both said almost simultaneously. I had a feeling the prank competition was stirring up bad blood between the partners. Frankly, the tension between those two was the least of my worries, though. How in the world was I going to get a town full of witches to stop using magic?

A far-off *boom* sounded. I looked at my Dad. "We need to get the word out to the community sooner rather than later, and maybe we should consider calling your mom."

Tanya groaned. "Do we have to?"

Dad rubbed his hand through his well-coiffed hair. His eyes crinkled with worry. "I'll take care of it, Hazel."

"Since there's no dead body for me to examine here, I'll help Kent with the witches," Tanya said.

I blinked at her. Did she just call my dad Kent? I noticed then that she was looking at him in the same way I'd seen her looking at Ford my first week back in town.

"Eww," I said. "He's old enough to be your father." In witch terms, that didn't mean much. My dad looked my age. But still!

Tanya's cheeks reddened. My dad took her by the arm. "Never mind." To me, he said, "I'll call you tonight."

Ford put his arms around me. "You should let me take you home. You need to rest if you are going to heal."

My ribs still hurt like a bitch, but I wasn't ready to give up on the day yet. "I need to talk to Agatha Milan. These fake legs might be harmless pranks, but it seems pretty elaborate and suspicious that someone keeps putting Agatha's clothes and shoes on the damn things."

As we walked back to his truck, a clown appeared, or rather, *the* clown, although something seemed different this time. Was he shorter?

"Ooga booga!" yelled the clown as he lifted up a blue plastic bucket. He launched its contents, and a cloud of pink glitter descended on us. Ford roared, and his face started to morph. The clown threw the bucket, which bounced off Ford's chest. Giggling madly, the clown ran away.

Glitter clung to my uniform, my hair, my eyelashes, and damn, even some had gotten into my mouth.

Ford looked like a pretty, pretty bear princess, but I refrained from laughing because he looked so miserable.

"The next time he shows up, you can shoot him," I said.

"If he shows up again, I'll rip him to rainbow-colored shreds." He frowned so hard it created creases at the corners of his mouth. "I hate clowns."

I was beginning to agree with him.

CHAPTER 7

After we had managed to get most of the glitter off ourselves, we tracked down Agatha Milan. Her home was on a three-acre plot in an older part of town that was known as Avalon. The upscale neighborhood had some of the original homes from when the town was first settled back in 1861 by the witches who had traveled from New England to escape persecution and get a fresh start.

They'd called the town Paradise Falls because of a small waterfall that spilled into a lake on the far side of the city borders. When I say small, I mean it's about twelve feet high. I remember my history teacher, Ms. Gedes, a witch who'd been born in Paradise Falls in 1868, said that the founding families, hers included, had believed the lake and the falls were on top of two powerful ley lines and would magnify their power.

There had been thirteen founders. A coven. Four witches died in the first year during some spell-gone-wrong. Nine members were left to carry on building the community. Ms. Gedes, who'd never married, had been proud of her mother. Back then they lived together in their own sedate version of *Grey Gardens*.

"I wonder if Ms. Gedes still teaches at the school," I said to Ford as we climbed the steps to the two-story Victorian Queen Anne home, gothic and lovely in its architecture.

The house was painted a buttery yellow and had a large covered porch, white columns, and an intricately carved front door. I could almost imagine sitting in an easy chair on the second-floor balcony and listening to the birds chirp away as I read a book. Goddess, there was oak, hazelnut, and pecan trees all over the place. Tizzy would be in nut heaven.

"What made you think of her?" asked Ford.

I knocked on the door. "I don't know. Just thinking about the town's history." I looked around. "I can't get over how big this yard is." The typical sounds of cars racing up and down the road were absent as well. "Or how quiet the neighborhood is."

"I think that's by design." Ford knocked this time,

louder, and I rang the doorbell. The tune "Do You Believe in Magic" began to chime inside the house.

"That's so awesome," I said.

Ford gave me a look that asked if I'd done gone and lost my mind. I shrugged. I liked what I liked.

A disheveled witch with purple hair opened the door. Her skin was surprisingly flawless. She had a sharp nose, a narrow face, a protruding thin chin, and high cheekbones. If she hadn't been beautiful, I would have called her classically witchy.

"What?" she asked. Her query had been ruder than I'd expected.

"Uhm, are you Agatha Milan?" Paradise Falls was a small town but not so small I knew all the residents by sight.

"Yes." Her answer was curt and annoyed.

Then Ford stepped forward. "Look, lady, we can have a friendly conversation here at your home, or we can do it downtown in a ten by ten interrogation room."

My mate was much better at charming people. Not. I'd underestimated just how much clown run-ins had put Ford on edge, but his tactic worked.

Agatha Milan backed up from the door and said, "Fine. Come in."

The interior was wall-to-wall hardwood floors. A fireplace in the living room had, what I imagined was, the original surround. Intricate woodwork accented everything. The white walls had a slight rose tint to them that gave the home an almost magical glow. When she escorted us into a sitting room lined with bookshelves, I sighed. "How good is business? This place is fantastic."

Agatha plopped down in one of the four leather chairs in the room. "It was my parent's house."

Inherited. No wonder. "I saw you downtown this morning. Did you see anything unusual before the event on Main Street?"

Her face pinched. "I didn't see anything."

For some reason, I didn't believe her. "Do you know why your clothes and shoes keep ending up on rubber legs around town?"

"What?" She seemed genuinely surprised.

"Twice now, there have been legs sticking out from under something. Dumpster lid, crumbling wall. And both times, articles that have been identified as matching your clothing and shoes were found on the legs and feet."

"Like the way the wicked witch was positioned when Dorothy's house fell on her," Ford said.

"Are you calling me a wicked witch?" Agatha demanded.

I stared at my mate as if he'd grown a second head.

Ford kept his gaze leveled at Agatha. "If the shoes fit."

Agatha's phone chirped. She pulled it from her pocket, her eyes widening when she saw the screen. It was simply a 5-5-5. "I have to take this." She left the room.

Ford and I looked around, and other than some tiny shards of broken glass on one of the bookshelves next to an old picture of a man, woman, and child, there was nothing out of the ordinary. Her taste in books seemed to follow mostly fashion and romance novels. I wished like hell I could cast a location spell for hidden secrets. Secrets I was certain Agatha kept. I'd most likely destroy this gorgeous house in the process, so I resisted the twitching impulse.

When Agatha returned, she said, "You have to leave. Now. Unless you plan to arrest me, I have nothing more to say to you."

When Ford and I were back out on the lawn and

walking toward the truck, he said, "That was ominous."

"Did you hear any of her phone conversation?"

"No," he said, "and not from a lack of trying. She went somewhere sound proof."

"That's suspicious."

"Or she just likes her privacy. I think almost every house in Paradise Falls has a quiet room. My parents turned their bedroom soundproof after I rushed in one night when I thought Dad was killing Mom?"

"What happened?"

He gave me a pointed look. "I walked in on my parents doing it, Hazel. That's what happened. After that, soundproofing was acquired." He shivered. "I still get nightmares."

"Clowns and parental sex."

"What?"

"I'm just trying to keep straight the things that freak you out. Why are you afraid of clowns?"

"I'm not," he said, but his hand drifted to his gun.

"Easy there, John Wayne."

"Can we stop talking about clowns and my parents sex life?"

I laughed. "In my defense, you brought up your parents."

He changed the subject. "Didn't you think there was something off about Agatha Milan? And why is the prankster targeting her? And why the sudden change in her demeanor after her phone call?"

I'd had those same questions, but unfortunately, none of the answers. Instead, I cackled at him in my best *Wizard of Oz* wicked witch impression and said, "I'll get you, my pretty. And your little dog too."

"Don't you mean squirrel?"

Awww. He thought of Tizzy as his too. It hit home just how much I really loved this man.

CHAPTER 8

At my insistence, Lily came over for dinner. I hated thinking of her alone in that house. At one point, I'd tried to talk her into moving in with us. We had three bedrooms and lots of space, but she said she liked her independence. I worried it wasn't healthy for her to stay in house with all the ghosts of her past. I mean, how can she move forward with her life when everything around her reminds her of what she's lost.

Ford cooked dinner, another reason in the long line of reasons that I loved him, and the pot roast smelled delicious. A shifter buddy of his, Troy Dancy, was an electrician, and he'd come over while we were putting out fires all over town and fixed the short in the wiring. It turned out the electrical problem had nothing to do with my coffee. Still. The hole in the center island and floor reminded us all that if the earth's rotation was thrown off because of an imbalance in the core, it was probably my fault. At least nothing had crawled up from the depths of hell through the hole. Yet.

Lily and Tizzy had been acting strange since their arrival, and when we sat down to eat, Tizzy said, "Show them, Lily."

"It was probably just a fluke." She brushed her unruly auburn hair back from her face and took a bite of roast. "Wow, Ford. This is excellent."

Tizzy clasped her hands excitedly. "Janet Strickland told you she'd been wearing the same panties for the past seven days!"

Now they had my attention. "How in the world did that come up?"

"We ran into Janet at the grocery store, and Lily told me her washing machine is broken, so she needed to get quarters for the laundry mat."

"Tizzy!" Lily glared at the squirrel then she looked at me. "It's not a big deal. It's just as easy to do the wash there as it is at home."

"You can bring your clothes here," I said. "I insist. Besides, it selfish on my part, because I get more time with you every week."

"So not the important part," Tizzy said, her voice heavy

with exasperation.

"This is not dinner conversation," Lily said. She looked at Ford. "Can you pass those mashed potatoes?"

Tizzy climbed up on the table and blurted, "Janet confessed that she hadn't had a working washer for a month, and that she'd been wearing the same underwear for a week!"

"No feet on the table during meals," Ford muttered. He didn't bother making it a command because Tizzy wouldn't obey anyhow.

"You guys don't get it," the squirrel chirped. "Lily is secret sniffer. People can't stop telling her things they wouldn't tell anyone about. Do it, Lily. Do it, do it, doo eeeet!"

Tizzy's insistence and Lily's reluctance made me curious. "What is she talking about, Lils?"

Exasperated, Lily put her knife and fork down. "It's nothing," she said. "I asked the grocer if her eggs were fresh, and she said she put them in new cartons because they were twelve days past the expiration date."

"Okay. Weird, but I'm not sure if that's a huge secret about it." The underwear thing, well, that was a whole 'nother story.

"You don't get it," Lily said. "She hadn't meant to tell me, Haze. But it was like she couldn't help herself. Just like Mike Dandridge with the clown confession and Janet revelation about her dirty underwear." Lily rubbed her face, looking more tired than I'd seen her in a long time. "This morning my neighbor John Decker was taking the trash out to the curb. I asked him about his wife. Instead of giving me the standard, 'She's doing okay. Getting there,' which has been his answer almost every day since their son Boyd died, he said, 'Terrible. Most days she's in bed. I worry one day I'll come home and find she's taken her own life.'" Lily stuttered out a heavy exhale.

"Yeah," Tizzy said. "And we tested it with other people. All the Shifters we asked questions answered us with whole truths. Even embarrassing questions."

Lily blushed. "I didn't want to ask personal questions, but I had to know. I had to ask things they wouldn't usually answer."

"What about witches?"

"It worked to some degree with witches and warlocks, unless the questions were too outrageous," Lily said. "They didn't lie about them, but they were able to withhold answers."

I remembered the feeling I had at the Tea Haus when

Lily had asked me about the investigation. The compulsion to answer her had been strong, and I only felt relief when I told her the truth. Was the magical black hole responsible for Lily's new ability?

Ford scoffed. "I find it hard to believe that Lily has some special power to make people confess. If that's the case, our jobs just got a whole lot easier."

I felt an evil smile tug the corners of my lips. "Fine. Lily, why don't you ask Ford why he's afraid of clowns."

"I'm not afraid of—"

"Why are you scared of clowns?" Lily asked him.

Ford immediately started talking. "When I was five years old, my father took me to the circus, and I snuck away to check out the clowns. They trapped me in their tiny car and tormented me for what felt like hours until my dad finally rescued me from the jesters of Satan." When he finished, his eyes widened as he clamped his mouth shut, his lips forming a thin line. He set down his silverware and stood up from the table. "I've lost my appetite."

"I'm sorry, Ford," Lily said.

Tizzy, who hadn't stopped laughing since the "jesters of Satan" line, was decidedly not sorry.

"Aww, Ford. That's terrible." I stood up to hug him, but he stepped out of reach.

He gave me a look that said he needed space. "I'm going to shower and wash the humiliation off me."

I wiggled my brows, trying to make things better with sexy-flirting. "Can I help?"

His spicy scent detonated my senses. Yum. He turned and headed for the stairs, with me following close on his heels.

"I'll get the dishes," Lily said.

"I'll supervise," Tizzy added.

I winked at Ford. "I'll be right up, lover."

As soon as he was up the stairs, I turned on Lily and Tiz. "There is something happening to the magic in this town. It's like every witch is turning into...well...me. Dad says spells are going awry all over Paradise Falls, just like at the Tea Haus kitchen. Maybe your new ability to compel the truth from folks is part of that magic?"

"I don't know," Lily said. "I didn't notice people wanting to tell me stuff until today, so I'm willing to operate as if the tar pit is doing something weird to me. Has any other shifters reported strange abilities?"

"Not so far, at least that I know of. I'll call the department later and see if they've had any calls." I worried my lower lip between teeth for a moment then said, "I have a bad feeling about this. I don't think that magical goo has anything to do with Prank Wars, which means, we have something sinister at work here in town."

Lily nodded. "I can ask around as well. I mean, I wouldn't have thought to report whatever is happening to me to the cops. Shifters tend to keep their personal stuff personal."

"Just don't make it to obvious or probative," I told her. "I don't want you getting hurt because you turned over the wrong can of worms."

"No worries," she said. "I'll be the epitome of discretion."

I heard the water kick in upstairs, reminding me that I had a hot date with a hot bear in a hot shower. I gave Lily a quick hug. "Come by for breakfast in the morning."

"You mean you want me to bring you over some donuts in the morning," she said.

I laughed. "Exactly."

CHAPTER 9

After a hot shower, followed by an even hotter make-out session, Ford and I cuddled in bed. The room was painted in warm browns and cool blues. The comforter covering the king-sized bed, any guy almost seven feet tall would require, was chocolate with light blue circles. I'd added some extra decorative pillows to the mix, but everything else in the room was Ford's aesthetic.

Unfortunately, no matter how many times he said the house was ours, I couldn't help but feel like it was his. His fingerprints were all over the décor. Sure, I'd added a few touches here or there, just little things to make me feel less like a guest, but I still didn't feel completely at home.

"Poor baby," I said, stroking Ford's broad hairy chest. I loved the way he looked in uniform, but I loved him out of uniform even more. "If another clown attacks you, I'll shove glitter dust right up his ass."

He plucked my hand off his chest and harrumphed. "It's not funny."

Since we were out of Tizzy's earshot, I said, "Yes, it is. Jesters of Satan." I snickered and put my hand back on his chest and twirled a small patch of chest hairs into a pretty swirl. "You are a big, bad bear Shifter. Beyond that, you are an officer of the law. Trained in self-defense. What can a clown, with his size seventeen feet, bicycle horn, and foam club do to you?"

"Those white-faced freaks with their squeaky red noses are as unnerving as they come." I felt him shudder.

To get his mind off clowns, I changed the subject. "That tar pit is pretty unnerving. I half-expected dinosaur bones to float to the surface."

Ford nodded his agreement. "I thought Matty Deerfield was going to have a stroke as his truck sank into the muck. I can't believe it completely disappeared under the surface."

"That truck was junk. I take it if Matty had money to replace it he would have done so already."

"There's a lot of grumbling in the shifter community that witches are responsible for the boiling, black gunk.

I hope the grumbling is wrong. Tanya took a sample back to her lab to analyze."

That name totally killed my afterglow. "Tanya took a sample, did she?"

Ford grasped my hand as I reflexively bunched his chest hairs into my fist. "Ouch." He brought my knuckles to his lips. "I've never wanted another woman the way I want you, Hazel. You are my mate. From now until I perish."

I relaxed my curled fingers. I sometimes forgot that shifters mated for life, unlike witches and warlocks who mated until it was inconvenient. Sometimes they did binding spells, to make the pairing permanent. It was a way to blend the magic and make the witch and warlock more powerful. Only problem was that once it was done it couldn't be undone, as my parents had learned the hard way. I prayed to the Goddess it wasn't so. Still, I couldn't help but think that he would have had a much different life if I hadn't drunkenly triggered his mating scent. What if I turned out to be a disappointment to him? Twenty years from now would Ford want to break his mating to me?

"I'm sorry," I said without elaborating.

He rolled sideways and gathered me in his arms. He branded me with a fiery kiss as I threaded my fingers through his thick, brown hair. Goddess, the man tasted as good as he smelled. I could give up desserts for the rest of my life as long as Ford Baylor always kissed me just like this.

His rumbly growl made me smile against his lips, and I could feel the solid log of his desire pressed against my hip. I chuckled and said, "There are no clowns in here, mister, so you can holster your gun."

He flipped me onto my back and pinned me beneath his massive body. I loved the way his heated skin felt against mine. He growled, raising shivers on my arms. "I'm planning on holstering this gun."

He pushed my thighs apart with his knees. I squawked with pleasure as a fine layer of perspiration formed on my chest and neck. I purred, "Oh, Officer Baylor, this is starting to feel a lot like police brutality." I wiggled my brows. "I like it."

He kissed my cheek, my neck, my… *brrrrring*! *Birrrrriiiiing*!

"No," I whined. "Not now." The caller screen showed the Paradise Falls Police Department phone number.

"Don't answer it," Ford said.

"It's the station, and it's eleven o'clock at night. It's probably important."

Ford let out a heavy sigh but didn't roll off me. He grabbed the phone off the nightstand. "It better be *city on fire* important."

He hit the green button on the screen and put the phone to my ear.

"Chief Kinsey," I said, as Ford kissed down my neck, his warm mouth on my breasts.

"We have a body, Chief," Officer Parker said.

Within a nanosecond, Ford was off my boobs, getting out of bed and pulling on his pants. Not an easy feat since his erection hadn't completely gone away. He winced as he tucked it down and zipped up his jeans. I mouthed the word, *sorry*, to him as he threw a pair of jeans and t-shirt at me.

I wondered why Parker was working. He'd been on day shift, so it didn't make sense that he'd be on call tonight. "Are you working overtime?"

"I am now," he said.

I put the phone on speaker and set it down while I dressed. Ford was dressed completely now and was putting on his socks. "Are you sure it's not just more rubber legs sticking out of something?"

"I checked. These ones have the rest of the body attached, Chief." His voice was solemn. "It's Agatha

Milan."

"What? Are you sure? We spoke to her this afternoon. Damn it. Where's the body located?"

"750 Elysium Street."

"Lolo's Diner?"

John Parker sounded angry when he spoke. "In the back dumpster."

"In another dumpster?" I shook my head as I snapped my bra into place. "We'll be there in fifteen. Secure the scene."

"Already in progress, Chief. I have two patrols on their way, and my partner Thomas is rounding up witnesses and taking statements."

"Good work," I told him. "Hold it down until I get there."

"What do you think?" Ford asked after Parker hung up. "Prank gone wrong?"

"I'm not sure any of the Agatha stuff was a prank." I remembered the look of panic and anger on her face when she'd kicked us out of her house. "Maybe they were warnings."

"We should get someone to run her phone," Ford said.

"That's a good idea. Hopefully, we'll know more when we get there."

"Should I call Tanya?" he asked.

My mood darkened even more. "No. I'll call her." It would be my gesture of an olive branch. I just hoped she didn't use it to beat me.

CHAPTER 10

Police cars, an ambulance, and a generous amount of town's folk occupied the front parking lot of Lolo's Diner. The diner's bright neon signs advertising burgers and shakes added to the pageantry. The place was open until midnight on weekends, which meant, it had been full of customers when the body had been discovered. How in the world had the killer or killers managed to get Agatha tucked away on a busy night without anyone noticing? Chances were, they hadn't.

John Parker waved at me when we got out of Ford's truck. He wore jeans and a leather jacket. Alice Michaels, a witch, and Rhonda Petry, a werecougar, my on-duty officers, were working the scene. They guarded the perimeter tape, keeping the crowd from going back behind the diner. The pair had been patrolling together for less than a month, so I was glad

Parker, a veteran cop, and his partner Mitzy Thomas had been on site.

When we reached Parker and Thomas, they led us around the backside. "Becksy Ansel found the body when she was taking the trash out." He shook his head and clenched his fist. "Luckily, we were here for dinner. She's pretty badly shaken, as you can imagine."

"We?" Maybe he and Thomas were figuring out a way to make their partnership work. I glanced back and forth between Parker and Thomas, and suddenly neither one of them wanted to meet my gaze. Uh oh. I shook my head. It wasn't a good idea for partners to mix work with their personal lives. Of course, I was the boss of my honey, so who was I to judge.

"Uhm. Well," Parker started.

I cut him off. The time for personal stuff was later. I recognized a young woman standing within the perimeter. "What's Becksy Ansel doing back here?" Becksy was a perky teenage witch who waitressed at the diner. She was efficient and had always struck me as responsible. "Have you taken her statement?"

John nodded. "We did."

Thomas added. "I called her dad and mom, too. They're on their way down to pick her up."

John gave me a look that dared me to reprimand them.

A low growl from Ford raised my brows.

"Is this personal for you, John?"

Before he could answer, Tanya came clacking on the scene in her four-inch-heels. "Is it really Agatha this time?" Her pale skin looked nearly gray. They must have been friends.

"I just arrived." I nodded toward Parker and Thomas. "They identified her when the body was discovered, but let's get it confirmed now."

The body had been laid out on a sheet on the ground. John or one of the other officers had placed a tarp over the corpse. I squatted down and pulled the tarp down to reveal Agatha's head.

Agatha's bright purple hair was matted and messy, not like the put together witch I'd seen this afternoon. Her dead eyes stared hollowly up at the sky. Her irises had gone milky.

Tanya gasped. "It's definitely her."

Parker nodded his agreement.

"Any apparent cause of death?" I asked.

"There's this," Parker said. He pulled the tarp up at her

feet, sliding it above her calf. An S, like the one on the rubber legs, had been carved into her flesh.

"Goddess," I breathed.

"Yep," said Parker, his eyes burning with rage. "Shifters."

"Now you don't know that for sure," Thomas said.

"What else could it mean?" Parker asked.

"You're jumping to conclusions, John," Ford said.

"Of course, you'd say that."

"What's that supposed to mean?" I heard the rising timbre in my mate's voice.

"You're one of them, so—" He let his words drop with just the implied accusation.

Whoa. Maybe I'd gotten it wrong about Parker and Thomas. The warlock didn't sound like someone having a fling with a therianthrope. The situation had suddenly become even dicier.

Ford took a step toward Parker, his shoulders squaring. Shifters loved a good fight, especially when they believed they were right. My man-bear was no exception.

"Parker," I snapped. "Go out front and help Petry and Michaels get statements."

He grunted his acknowledgment but didn't take his eyes off Ford. Really bad idea.

"Hey!" I shouted. Parker whipped his gaze to me. I pointed my finger at him. "Do you need some time off?"

His angry expression eased. "I...I...no, Chief. I don't need any time off."

"Then get your head into police work and out of politics. We don't have enough evidence to accuse a gnat of buzzing the corpse and certainly not enough to blame half our community for this death based on one single letter. If I hear one whisper of anti-shifter sentiment because you're talking out turn, you'll be doing more than taking some time off. You'll be finding another job."

Parker was staring at his feet now, his jaw working back and forth.

I glared at him, putting the full-force of my conviction into my words. "Do you understand me, Officer Parker?"

"Yes, Chief," he said sullenly. "I understand."

"Good. Now go make yourself useful, and for Goddess sake, don't taint the investigation with your prejudice."

He turned on his heels and marched around the front of the building.

"I could have handled him," Ford said.

"And then I'd have had to dress down two of my officers tonight." I waved my hand at him. "One was plenty, thank you very much."

I glanced at Mitzy. Her shoulders sagged. "He's not usually like this, Chief. I think this week is just getting to him."

"If he puts my investigation in jeopardy because he can't reign in his prejudices, he'll be out of a job. Make sure he knows that I'm not messing around."

She nodded. "I will."

"Good, now you go keep an eye on your hothead partner."

Mitzy walked off, leaving me with Ford, Tanya, and the very dead Agatha Milan.

"Could it be Shifters?" Tanya said as she did a quick examination of the body.

I hoped not but it was too early to rule anyone out. "You're the medical examiner. You tell me."

She waved at the ambulance drivers to collect the victim. "I'll do a full autopsy tonight and get back to you tomorrow with my preliminary findings."

"Thanks," I said. I hated to admit it, but I was grateful for Tanya's ability to separate her emotion from her work. She was obviously distraught over Agatha's murder, but she hadn't jumped to any wild conclusions. "I mean it."

She quirked her eyebrow up as if waiting for follow-up sarcasm, and when none came, she nodded. "I'll call you when I have something."

After the ambulance had taken Agatha Milan, Tanya followed them to the hospital in her car. Ford and I went back to the dumpster.

"I'm going to use an evidence location spell while the scene is fresh," I said. It was the one and only spell I'd mastered over the years, and I could do it without any real effort.

"Do you think that's a good idea?" Ford asked.

"Probably not." But what was the worst that could happen? It wasn't like I could burn a hole to China or anything. Right. "You might want to stand around the corner just in case."

My mate, who wasn't a stupid man, walked away to stand on the other side of the corner.

I paced the perimeter of the large trash bin and incanted my second sight spell.

"Goddess bring me second sight.

Turn any evidence into light.

A crime is done, most obscene.

Reveal hidden truths, unseen seen.

Done is done, Goddess grant to me,

Second sight, so mote it be."

For a brief moment, nothing happened, but then the whole area lit up with a rainbow of colors.

"What is this?" I whispered as the power swam around me. I'd never seen so much raw magic in one area. The overlapping blues, greens, purples, yellows, and reds obscured my ability to discern anything helpful for finding Agatha's killer.

The magic grew thick, almost choking as it tugged at my own power. Four shadows rose through the auras, wrapping and twisting. I could almost hear chanting beneath the loud hum of energy, and it felt as if the blood in my veins burned. My skin went taut and I worried it would split me wide open. I bit back a scream and tried to end my spell with a quick:

"*Second sight, go away.*

You're too bright.

Get away from me.

So mote it be."

The area went completely still as if frozen in time. Without warning, a quiet peal of laughter broke the silence and sent chills down my spine. One by one the shadows punched their way through my body. I could hear them talk, I could feel their desires for power, and I could see the world it had once been for them. The buildings disappeared around me. No longer was I standing in the back of Lolo's. Now I was in a small room. Wooden benches lined the walls, but the floor was clear of any furniture.

Thirteen women stood in a circle, their hands clasped as they chanted. "*Macht, die, komm zu mir sein.*" Over and over, the same words. I didn't understand them, but I understood the intensity of the spell they were performing as it threatened to choke me.

A deafening *boom*, followed by the ground shaking, and the roof falling in, finally stopped their spellcasting. When the dust cleared, I witnessed nine of the thirteen get up while four of their sisters lay crumpled and dead on the wooden floor.

Two strong arms wrapped around me, and I could hear my name being repeated. I struggled to regain control of my mind and body, to chase the shadows away. The cold night air hit me with such force as I inhaled a gasping breath and sagged into Ford's arms. I reeled from the implications of the vision.

"Are you okay? What happened?"

"Ghosts," I said. And not just any ghosts, witch-ghosts." I was afraid to put into words what I knew from the glimpse into the past to be true. Someone had cast a summoning spell and called forth four dead witches.

CHAPTER 11

"I thought we agreed on a magic ban," my father scolded me for the umpteenth time. I felt like a teenager again. "That means for everyone, even you."

I'd called him from the truck and told him to get the Shifter-Witch Council down to the coalition office. And I was quickly regretting my decision. He and Tanya had arrived first. Oh, joy of joy.

"I know," I said. I wasn't trying to create anything, so I really hadn't expected it to go so horribly wrong. "But the good news is that we know what we're dealing with now, maybe. Right?"

"Wrong," Tanya replied. "Witches don't become ghosts unless they are summoned, and if these were the four witches from the original coven who died, then we are in deep dog poop here."

Her language surprised me. It made Tanya seem almost like a normal person. Ugh. She was my nemesis, I didn't want to think of her like she was normal.

"The witches were chanting something like *mack die come zoo der zeen*, or something like that," I said.

"My babble to English translation is rough, but it sounds like German. A power spell, by the sound of it," Dad said.

"Look, I'm sorry I can't be more accurate. I was a little freaked out when I was sucked into that vision of the past. It was too much like I was there. Way too real."

My father gave me a solemn look. "I suppose it's lucky we know anything at all at this point."

"Right? If I hadn't broken the ban, we would still be in the dark."

He didn't bother with a response.

Bryant Baylor, Mary Lowe, and Steve Crandell arrived at the coalition office a few minutes later, and I had to tell the story all over again. Each of them looked at me as if I were the cause of all the gloom and doom.

I threw up my hands. "I didn't summon those stupid witches or that monstrous sucking hole in the middle of downtown! Sheesh, shoot the messenger much."

"Well, whoever did it has unleashed a big can of whoop-ass on the town," Bryant said. "I've never seen so many disasters happen all at once."

Again, it felt like an indictment. "Yeah, it's not like anything bad ever happened in Paradise Falls before I arrived." I resisted sticking my tongue out at my mate's dad. "Again, I say, I didn't freaking summon the dead witches."

Though, I had a suspicion it was definitely witches that started this kerfuffle. With Adele Adams gone, it made the other witches braver. She had been a psychopathic, homicidal maniac, but she had also been mad powerful, which helped to keep the other witches in town in check.

As if thinking of crazy powerful had conjured crazy powerful, a gray puff of smoke filled the center of the room, followed by Tanya groaning, "Oh, no," and a woman in a white power suit, silver hair appeared where the smoke had been.

"Grand Inquisitor," my father said formally with a slight bow of his head. My heart hurt for him. As much as I wanted to be mad at him for leaving, I imagined he had to be as mad at his mother for taking him away.

"Who is this?" Steve Crandell asked.

Mary Lowe, leader of the big cats, whacked him, so I

didn't have to. "Have some respect," she said. "That's Grand Inquisitor Clementine Battles, and she does not mess around."

"Grandmother," I said.

"Hello, Hazel. It's good to see you." She looked around the room at the rest of the coalition including Steve, Mary, and Bryant. She gave my dad, Tanya, and me a quick nod before getting down to business. "You all have a big problem here in Paradise Falls."

"No shit," I muttered.

Tanya's eyes bugged at me.

"Sorry," I added quickly. "I mean, yes, you're absolutely right. We have a big problem. Well, several big problems."

"Whoever summoned the ghosts has unleashed them on your town without any real knowledge of how it would affect the natural energy this place holds," The Grand Inquisitor said. She looked at my father. "Hello, Kent."

He grimaced. "Hello, Mother."

"How do we fix this?" Mary asked. She was generally a quiet woman, but when she did speak it was usually to the point. I dug that about her.

Steve, the newest member of the coalition, said, "I've had trucks adding gravel to that black hole all day, and I'm going to run out of rocks before it ever filled in."

"That's because it's a hellmouth," The Grand Inquisitor said.

"A what-mouth?" Bryant asked.

"A hellmouth," she repeated, only more slowly and with a lot of enunciation.

"As in a Sunnydale kind of hellmouth?" I asked. "Where's Buffy the ghost-witch slayer when you need her?"

"Or is it more like the Supernatural kind of hell-mouth?" Tanya said.

Nooooo, Tanya, don't be cool. Damnit. My nemesis was making me reevaluate my feelings for her. I smiled in her direction. "I could use a hug from the Winchester boys about now."

"The hell you could," Ford grumbled.

"I meant that metaphorically," I said. To Tanya, I mouthed the words, *No, I didn't.*

She smiled and shook her head.

"You're both in the ballpark," The Grand Inquisitor said.

"Is that why all the magic is Revelation-ary?"

"Yes. The magic around here is always heightened near Samhain, which is why the non-magic prank competition began over a hundred years ago. It was a way to get the witches in town to focus their excess energy on things that wouldn't kill them."

I gave her and assessing stare. Had she been around when the town was founded?

"Wow. How come that wasn't taught in school?" Tanya asked. "I might have paid more attention to local history."

The Grand Inquisitor ignored her. "First thing you need to do is track down the witches who cast the summoning."

"There're only about four thousand witches in town," I said. "No problem."

The Battle-axe wrinkled her nose at me. "I think we can narrow it down some. It has to be descendants from the original coven of thirteen. I believe there are thirty-one living here in town."

"You wouldn't happen to have that list handy, would you?" my dad asked.

My grandmother scowled at him, but he managed not to turn into a toad.

"Oh, I think I might know where to find one!" I looked at Ford. "Ms. Gedes."

"The history teacher," Tanya said.

"Yes, her mother is one of the founding members. Remember how she had that chart she used in class to trace the genealogy of the original witches?"

"Goddess, you're right." She smiled, and then realized who she was talking to, and added, "Even a dog finds a bone every once in a while."

"Are you calling me a bitch?"

The corners of her mouth curved upward into a grin. "Maybe."

Was Tanya giving me banter? The world really was coming to an end. "Should we call, Ms. Gedes or just drive over to get the document?"

The Grand Inquisitor sparkled out and, in a few minutes, returned with a piece of parchment in hand. "That woman is highly organized," she said with admiration. She gave the list to my Dad. "Call everyone on this list and have them meet us at the hellmouth."

My dad's lips pressed into a thin line. I knew he'd had enough of being her lackey to last two lifetimes, but he finally nodded.

I peered over his shoulder to get a look at the names, and one of them made my stomach drop and my mouth dry. "Why is Lily Mason on the list? She's a shifter, not a witch?"

My grandmother narrowed her gaze on me. "Oh, come now, Hazel. Do you really believe that you and Ford invented love between a shifter and a witch." She pointed to Lily's line. It had her name across from Danny's, and above her was her mom, Constance Mason, deceased, her dad, Jack Mason, deceased, and across from Jack was the name Daniel Mason, where-abouts unknown, with a birth date all wrong to be her brother Danny twice.

"Who is that?" I said, pointing at the name.

"I would assume it's Jack Mason's brother," my grandma said. "And if you follow there line up, you'll see that the line eventually lands on Liliana Grace.

"Wait a minute," I said. "Lilianna Grace? She's one of the founding coven members. So you're trying to tell me that Lily has witch blood in her family tree?"

"I'm not trying, dear," my grandmother said. "I think I'm being perfectly clear with my words."

"But Liliana died. She was one of the four who didn't survive the power spell. One of the ghosts."

"Yes," she said.

Then it dawned on me. If Lily was a descendant of the original thirteen, maybe the Grand Inquisitor thought she was somehow involved. "You can't believe that Lily has anything to do with the summoning."

"Of course not."

"Good." Because I might be able to forgive her for taking my father away, but I'd never forgive her if anything bad happened to Lily. "What does this mean for her?"

Grandma smiled reassuringly. "She was born a shifter, my dearest child. It means nothing for your friend. She has no magic, so that makes her relatively harmless."

I kept Lily's newly found abilities to myself. She was off the Grand Inquisitor's radar, and that's exactly where I wanted her to stay.

My dad was still looking at the list. "How in the world am I supposed to contact all these people tonight without using magic?"

"You're a resourceful boy," his mother said. "I'm sure you'll come up with a remarkable plan."

Tanya put her hand on his arm. "I'll help you," she said.

Again, Tanya with the goo-goo eyes at my dad. Sheesh. I did not want Tanya Gellar to be my new mommy. Wah!

"And what would you like me to do?" I asked.

"Do what you do. Investigate." She gave me a look that made me both curious and anxious. "When your father gather's all the founding witch descendants, we will have to meet at the hellmouth at eleven-thirty tonight, right before the witching hour. It will be the best time to undo whatever has been done. But none of it will do us any good if we can't find out who's responsible. That's your job."

Great, I thought. Why didn't she give me something easy to do? Like bring about world peace. "I'll do my best."

"I know you will."

"Do you think we can? Fix it, I mean?"

She patted my cheek. "Goddess willing."

CHAPTER 12

F ord and I slept a couple of hours before rolling out of bed at six in the morning. He went into the office to check on any unusual reports beyond the murder and the hell mouth, to see what we could tie into this bigger incident. I'd put my police force on alert after the meeting ended at three a.m. I didn't know how I was going to figure out the culprits before midnight, but I had bigger fish to fry this morning.

Lily was coming over with donuts, and I had to decide how much of last night I wanted to tell her. She believed her entire family was gone, and according to record, she wasn't completely wrong. Her parents, her grandparents, and all the way back to Liliana Grace had been listed as deceased. All of them except for Daniel Mason, whereabouts unknown. I didn't want to get her hopes up about a long-lost family member if it turned out he was dead as well. I mean, he had been Jack's brother. It seems like Lily would have known about an uncle if he still existed. No, I wouldn't tell her about him. Not yet. At least not until I could track down the address of his home or his grave.

Telling her about the witch in her family closet, well, that was a different story.

"Hazel, I'm here," Lily said as she walked in. "I hope you're up because I've got hazelnut coffee as well."

I smiled as Tizzy skidded out of her room and into the kitchen. "I love hazelnut!"

Lily put the box of donuts down, along with the drink carrier holding two large covered cups and one small. "I didn't forget about you, Tisiphone," she said. "I even got you a donut with candied pecans."

Tizzy flopped onto her back in a fit of bliss. "You're the best, Lils!"

"You really are," I agreed.

"Why are you dressed already?" Lily asked. "I know you didn't put a bra on for me, so what's up?"

I felt the same compulsion that I'd felt at the Tea Haus. "You need to reign your mojo in," I told her, trying hard not to blurt out that she had an uncle out there somewhere.

She blushed. "I'm sorry, Haze. I wasn't trying to..."

"I know you weren't." I smiled. "By the way, I think I might know where your new trick comes from."

"Well, don't keep me hanging."

"I won't know for sure until we do a little research, but I found out last night that your great, great grandmother was a founding witch in Paradise Falls."

She blanched. "Get out. That can't be true. I think I would have known something like that."

Well, she didn't know her dad had a brother, so... "Well, according to the records that Ms. Gedes kept on the thirteen witches and their families, you are a direct descendent on your dad's side. Liliana Grace had a baby with a shifter. He's not mentioned, and since she is one of the four witches who died--"

"Wait a minute," she said. "Who died?"

Oh, right. I hadn't told her about Agatha Milan or the ghosts or any of it. "Boy, a lot happened after you went home last night."

"I thought you were going to get a little nookie and go to bed?"

I half-smiled. "That definitely happened. But then I got a call from John Parker." I relayed the events of the night from Lolo's diner, the vision of the past, and everything that took place at the coalition meeting, minus the uncle thing.

When I was done, Lily stood up. "Well, get your purse, Gert. Looks like we're going on a witch hunt."

GOLDA GEDES HOME WAS IN THE SAME AREA AS AGATHA Milan's place. Her house was Victorian in style, but less gothic then Agatha's place. There was a luxury four-door sedan in the driveway when we pulled in.

When I parked the car and turned it off, Lily said, "After this we should go visit Agatha's house."

I gave her an "Are you crazy?" look.

"I may be a poor excuse for a shifter, Hazel, but I have a really good nose. I might be able to pick up on something there. Besides, the house is empty, so what harm could it do to go have a look around."

"What if she's put magical booby traps around her doors or something?"

"The way you tell it, if there are magical traps then they have been triggered. And since the house was still standing when we went by, I'd say it's probably safe."

A snicker from the back seat made me glower.

"She got you good, Haze," Tizzy said.

"You hush," I told her. "It's not too late for me to send you home."

"I am staying," Tiz said. "Lily is my friend, too, and I want to know what's going on with her as much as you do." I could hear the worry in my familiar's voice, and it softened my edges.

Lily cast an affectionate smile in Tizzy's direction. "That settles it," she said, and we exited the car.

Ms. Gedes door wasn't nearly as ornate as Agatha's had been, but it was made of rich mahogany and looked like it cost as much as my whole month's salary. I rang the doorbell, and deep, low chimes played a lyrical Irish Eire should had played for her students when we took tests.

A few second later, she opened the door. I'd spent so much time among humans, that I half expected Ms. Gedes to have a few wrinkles or graying hair, but she still looked like she had all those years ago, brown hair, soft and voluminous, kind eyes, and lovely smooth skin. She was curvier than most witches, but to me, her curves made her even more beautiful.

"Can I help you?" she asked.

"Hi, Ms. Gedes," I said. "I hope you don't mind us stopping by."

"Do I know you?" Her gaze shifted to Tizzy, and she smiled. "Hazel Kinsey. It has been a long time." She looked at Lily next. "Lily Mason. I see you two are still joined at the hip. Come on in." She led us through the foyer to a sitting room. "Can I get you a cup of tea or something?"

"No, thanks, ma'am," I answered. I was on a time crunch. "I need some information on the town founders, if you wouldn't mind talking to us about them."

"I'm always in the mood to teach a history lesson," she said. "Please have a seat. I'm going to get my cup of tea from the kitchen. Are you sure you don't want any?"

We all shook our head, and she left us to fetch her drink.

The sitting room was stacked with books, maps, and all sorts of historical-looking relics. "I'm going to go look around," Tizzy whispered in my ear. "You keep the old lady distracted."

She was over a hundred-years-old, but by human standards, Ms. Gedes looked no older than her late thirties, early forties at most. Definitely not old-looking, but I knew what Tizzy meant. "Don't break anything." I really didn't expect Tizzy to find anything important, but I thought her snooping might keep her distracted for a few minutes, so I could get the information I came for.

Ms. Gedes sat in a high back velvet cushioned chair across from Lily and me. The loveseat was functional and decorative, but not super comfy. "What can I do for you girls?"

"Can you tell me about Liliana Grace?"

Ms. Gedes let a small slip of smile tug at her lips. "My mother used to talk about Liliana. She was very powerful. Her magic was one of the most feared among the thirteen."

"Why?" I asked.

"Rumor has it, Liliana was the reason they all had to run from Connecticut." She set her tea down.

"Our ancestors came from Connecticut?" This was a new one on me.

"Not yours, Hazel. Your family came later to Paradise Falls." She raised her brows at my BFF. "But Lily, well, yes, I guess part of her family came from Connecticut."

"You know that she's Liliana Grace's descendent?"

"Of course, who do you think keeps the books. You

know, the ones your grandmother took from my house last night." I detected only mild irritation in her tone. "She promised to bring them back, Hazel. I will hold you to her word."

"Yes, ma'am," I said. "I'll make sure you get them back." I leaned forward. "So what was this ability of Liliana's that got her and the coven into enough trouble to drive them from their homes?"

"Why, Liliana could make the devil himself, the author of lies, tell the truth. No one could resist her magic. She took spells from other covens and acquired them for hers, this was as taboo now as it was then. It wasn't just the human's our original coven ran from."

That answered the why of Lily's new abilities, but it didn't answer the how.

Lily spoke up. "Can I have some latent ability of hers?"

Ms. Gedes lowered her brows and peered at Lily as if examining a rare artifact. "I felt that," she said. "Though it shouldn't be possible. Shifters and witches can cross breed, but the child is always one or the other, never both." She got up. "May I touch you?"

Lily nodded, but I kept a wary eye on the older witch. I didn't want to believe she could be involved in the current mess, but I also didn't want risk Lily's life by being dumb.

Ms. Gedes took Lily's hand.

"Don't do any magic," I told her. "It's unpredictable right now."

She nodded. "I got the memo." She turned her attention back to Lily. "My family has a talent for finding magic. It's what made my mother such a valuable asset to the coven. All thirteen witches were some of the most powerful in the country because of her. She brought in every one of them, including your grandmother." She brought Lily's hand to her chest. "If you'll indulge me for just a moment. My gift is not as strong as my mother's and it takes me a few seconds to make it work."

I watched the two of them, Lily staring at our history teacher as Ms. Gedes, eyes closed, took deep breaths as she clutched my friends hand. Finally, she let go and opened her peepers.

"It's there," she said. "But it's a kernel. An ability, like mine, that doesn't require spell work." She smiled. "How exciting to have a piece of Liliana Grace live on in this place."

"You can't tell anyone," I said.

"You extracted no such promise from me, young Kinsey."

"Will you tell anyone?" Lily asked. I felt the weight of her question.

Ms. Gedes shook her head. "I will keep your secret," she said. "For as long as it suits me."

Witches, I thought. Always angling. "Have you heard about what's going on in the middle of town?"

"I stay away from all populated areas during Halloween week," she said. "I didn't like Prank Wars as a teenager, and I don't like them now, no matter how necessary. Did something happen I should be aware of?"

"Only if you care that a hellmouth as been opened on Main Street and four founding ghosts have been summoned to Paradise Falls?"

"For Goddess sake," she said. "What can I do to help?"

"My dad is rounding up all the founding families, and he will be bringing them to the hellmouth tonight before witching hour."

"I suppose this was the Grand Inquisitor's plan," Ms. Gedes said.

"You suppose right, but I still need to figure out who summoned the ghosts and conjured the hellmouth before then." In the next room over a whip of movement caught my eye. I nearly swallowed my tongue when I saw Tizzy swinging the end of a brass floor lamp as it crashed to the floor. "Dear Goddess," I moaned.

Ms. Gedes didn't turn around. "Tisiphone, come in her now unless you want detention."

Tizzy skittered into the room, her nails clicking on the hardwood floors. "I'm here," she said.

"I'm afraid, that other than showing up tonight to help banish the hellmouth, I'm not much help," she told me. "I keep to myself. Even when Jenny Weaver asked me to join the Founders Society, I said no."

"Did you know she shoots blue sparkles from her butt when she toots?" Tizzy asked.

Ms. Gedes smiled. "One of the many reasons I turned her down."

CHAPTER 13

I didn't ring the doorbell to Agatha's house. Since I couldn't use magic, I used my mundane lock-picking skills, something I'd learned to do at Quantico, to get us through the front door.

"This place is off the chain! It's like *Addam's Family Values* meets *The Age of Innocence*," Tizzy said, referencing two movies she liked.

"Let me know if either of you see a cell phone," I told them both. "Agatha's phone wasn't on her person last night. So, either the killer took it, or it's somewhere in the house."

Lily nodded, but Tizzy had already scurried up the stairs. "You should see these bedrooms," she squeaked loudly. "They are ginormous."

"Look for something helpful, Tiz!" I yelled up the stairs

before heading the direction I'd seen Agatha go yesterday afternoon when she'd received the phone call.

"I'll take the kitchen first," Lily said, and we all split up to search.

I found the quiet room, as Ford had called it. Unfortunately, it looked like someone had gotten there before me. A file cabinet, a desk, and bookshelves were opened and disheveled. Either Agatha was the untidiest witch I'd ever met, or her place had been ransacked. Weirdly, the rest of the house hadn't been tossed like this room. This had to be where she kept anything of interest.

"Lils," I called from the door. "I need you."

The smell of cinnamon preceded Ford as he walked into the room. "What are you doing here?"

"What are you doing here?" I asked.

"I thought I'd bring a crew to check out Milan's house for evidence, but it looks like you and your crew beat me to it."

I rose up on my tip toes and kissed him. "Rank has its privilege."

Lily came up behind him. "I haven't found a thing," she said. "You?"

"Just a trashed room." I gestured to the chaos. "There's no way of telling if they took all the evidence or if anything was left behind we can use to track down the perps."

Lily's claws extended from her finger tips and her nose took on a more cat-like shape. She got closer to the mess and sniffed around the entire place. "I definitely smell four distinct signatures in here," she said.

"Can you identify who they belong to?"

She shook her head. "Maybe if I could get in a room with the suspects, I could tell you, but right now, they are distinguishing without having any real meaning for me."

"Ford? Can you tell who the scents belong to?"

He studied the room, going over every inch that Lily had covered. "All I can smell is vanilla and rum," he said.

"Oh, boy." My mating scent had fouled the room. "What if I leave?"

"I'll still only smell you." He crossed his arms. "I think Lily should come with us to this thing your grandmother set up for tonight."

"I don't want her a hundred miles of whatever the

Grand Inquisitor has planned for tonight," I said. "Things are going to get even more dangerous."

"I can decide for myself," Lily said. "If you think founding families are involved and they will all be there tonight, then it makes sense that I should go."

"Lily, no." I glared at Ford. He gave a slight nod of his head. "We can do this without you."

She steeled her expression. "But the point is, you don't have to. Besides, my new ability might come in handy as well. Even if the witches can resist my charm, I get this weird feeling one someone isn't being truthful."

"Like a human lie detector," I said.

"Like a not-human-at-all lie detector," she corrected.

"I don't like it."

She smiled. "I'll make a note of it."

"I found something!" Tizzy squealed from the bannister. "Come quick!"

We all raced up the stairs after her and followed her past two large bedrooms and a bathroom to a double door at the end of the hall that led to a huge master bedroom. The room was done in burgundies, dark greens, and golds. A queen-sized four-poster bed with velvet curtains pulled back to expose a gold and burgundy comforter. Agatha took gothic romance to a whole new level. I have expected Lord Byron to come sauntering into the room. Other than a fancy bedroom, though, I couldn't see anything of interest.

"In here," Tizzy said, pointing to a partially opened door on the far side of the room.

I opened the door and gaped. "What the fudge?" Inside was a statue of a woman with a gold wreath on her head. Melted candles, cards, beads, and other trinkets surrounded her feet. "Is that supposed to be the Goddess?"

"A goddess," Tizzy said. "You really are a terrible witch." My familiar shook her judgmental head at me. "It's Circe."

"Okay?" The name sounded like something I'd heard before, but it didn't hold any real significance for me. "Who's Circe?"

"Only the first witch," she said. "Sheesh, your dense."

"And your about to forage for you own nuts for the winter," I countered.

"Fine." She threw up her paws. "Circe is touted as the first witch. The one and only original. The first woman blessed by the Goddess. The queen--"

"I get it. She was magic before magic was cool." I looked at the statue. "Why is this significant?"

"If you look at the cards, you'll see they are all Tarot. Agatha was worried, as well she should have been. She had been burning white candles and offering gifts to Circe, the mother of magic." When I looked less than impressed. She grabbed up the four cards and handed them to me.

On the fronts were the same symbol that had been carved into Agatha's leg, only each one had come from a different deck. Only, the S's were more like lightning bolts striking over different kinds of tall buildings.

"Those are Tower cards," Lily said.

"How do you know about Tarot?" I asked.

"I dabbled a little after you left." She shrugged. "No biggie. It's not like any of the predictions came true. I don't have the magic for it."

"What does the Tower mean?"

"Danger," Tizzy said. "Extreme danger. I think she tried to read her future from four different decks, and each one predicted that her house of cards was about to come tumbling down."

I turned the cards over and noticed tiny scrawls of lettering in the corners. "Wait." I put one of them closer to the light. It had a J in the corner. Another had an R. There was also an A on the third, and a R on the fourth. "Jara? Raja?" I said aloud. "Did you see some kind of container in here?" I asked Tiz.

She shook her head. "No."

"Hmmm." I shoved the cards in my pocket. "Is there anything else?"

"Not that I saw," Tiz said.

"Nothing in the rooms where I looked," Lily agreed.

"Lily, can you take Tizzy home?"

"Sure," she said. "Where are you going next?"

I put my hand on my hunky mate's chest. "To a place I never want to go."

Ford covered my hand with his. "Off to see a medical examiner about a body."

TANYA WORE A WHITE LAB COAT AS SHE TYPED UP NOTES in her office. She waved at Ford and me to come inside.

"I would have called with my findings," she said. "I've only made a preliminary exam. Things are going a little more slowly since I can't use my magic."

"Welcome to my world."

She gave me a sour look. "You chose not to use your magic. It's not the same thing."

"If you call blowing myself up versus not blowing myself up a choice, I concede your point."

Tanya unexpectedly chuckled. "Let me show you what I've discovered so far. She pulled a picture of Agatha's leg and the two rubber ones out of a folder. "Do you notice the difference?"

Ford shook his head. "They all look the same to me."

I spotted the one not like the others right off the bat. "Agatha's lightning bolt is upside down, or right side up, as the case may be."

"You got it," Tanya said. "And I'd taken fingerprints from the fake legs, but hadn't run them because we were operating on the probability that they were pranks, but I ran them this morning, you know, after Agatha..." She shook her head, then pulled a tissue from a box on her desk and blew her nose."

"Were you close?"

"I am a descendent of a founding witch," she said. "Agatha was a mentor to me over the years."

"Were you part of the Founders Society?" I asked,

remembering Ms. Gedes saying that she'd been asked by Jenny Weaver.

She tucked her chin, her shoulders rising slightly. "How do you know about the FS?"

I looked at Ford. He shrugged.

"Is it some kind of secret club? Like the Masons or something?"

"It's nothing sinister," she said. "We meet once a year, plus we give each other deals on stuff. Like Agatha sold me clothes at a big discount, and I did the same with regular medical visits for members. It's a way to get a leg up in town. We help each other out."

"Who all is in this club of yours?"

She stared at me for a moment, then shook her head. "I can't tell you. It's against member rules."

"How about if I arrest you for obstruction?" I asked her as all the reasons I disliked this woman came back to me.

"Now, Hazel," Ford said. "Calm down."

"Do you know how to get a woman to go off on you?" I asked him. "You tell her to calm down."

He held his hands up and looked at Tanya. "Sorry.

You're on your own here. If I were you, I'd answer the question."

"Then I guess she'll have to arrest me," she said. "Now do you want to hear what I found out with the finger-prints, or do you put me in cuffs now?"

"The cuffs can wait." In a way, I admired her loyalty. "What did you find out?"

"Both fake legs had one set of fingerprints on them. Agatha's. I think the rubber legs came from her display models at her clothing shop." She pointed to the light-ning symbol on Agatha's real leg. "It's upside down."

"Because she carved it herself," I said.

"Yes!" Tanya smacked her desk with excitement then quickly composed herself. "I think she did it to herself."

"But why?"

"That's your field of expertise," Tanya said. "I give you the what, and you get to figure out the who and why."

I narrowed my gaze on her. "Are you dating my dad?"

She shifted uncomfortably in her seat as Ford backed out of the room. Coward.

Tanya met my gaze. "Kent and I have been seeing each other."

"Is that fancy speak for dating?"

"Among other things."

"Gross."

She smiled. "Don't ask the questions if you don't want the answers."

I gave her a quick nod. "I'll be back later to arrest you."

She gave me a one finger wave. "You know how to find me."

CHAPTER 14

We drew a big zero for the rest of the day. None of the reports coming in gave us any new information on the case. My grandmother gave me one job, to find the witches who started it all. I was pretty sure I knew who one of them was. Agatha Milan. I don't know why she was carving the Tower symbol into dummy legs, or why she would do it to her own, but I was fairly confident she'd been part of the group who'd summoned the ghosts and opened the hell-mouth. Interviewing witnesses had gotten us nowhere, so I'd spent my evening, along with most of my police force, rounding up founding families to make sure they weren't late for the Grand Inquisitor's grand finale.

Ford parked the truck a block over from Bliss and Main Street, it was nearly eleven-thirty and I didn't want to be on my grandmother's bad side for being tardy. The three-quarter moon lit the clear October sky, of course, and all I wanted to do was go home, crawl into bed, and act like the last two days hadn't happened.

Tizzy and Lily exited from the passenger side. We'd all squeezed in the front, but since Tizzy and Lily both had narrow booties, it hadn't been difficult.

"You don't think Clementine will be mad that I'm here, do you?" Lily said. Anxiety and tension pinched her expression.

"Clementine, huh?" Tizzy asked. "You're on a first-name basis with witch boogie monster."

"We spent some time together when she took me to Tanya to get healed."

"I think you'll be okay. If she's letting you call her Clementine, you'll probably fare better than I will," I said.

There were men in black circling a group of men and women who looked frightened, angry, and tired. I sympathized. But someone had started this mess, and it was threatening to destroy the town, so they could all suck it up.

Speaking of the Battle-axe. Grandma Grand Inquisitor sauntered up to us, her four-inch heels softly clicking on the concrete sidewalk. "Lily, it's so lovely to see you." She embraced my bestie as if they were long lost siblings. "You look beautiful."

"Thanks, Clementine." Lily smiled. "You look really nice too."

The Grand Inquisitor beamed.

Ugh. I tried not to lose my shit. "Lily got a good whiff of some possible suspects at Agatha Milan's house. I need her to smell the folks we gathered here to see if any of them match," I explained. Not that I needed to. Grandmother seemed fine with Lily's presence.

"Have you been experiencing any unusual side effects to the increase in magic, Lily?" the Grand Inquisitor asked.

"Rut roh, Rooby," I murmured to Lily.

She rolled her eyes at me. "It's fine," she said. "We should tell her."

"What if she kidnaps you for experiments," I said.

"Hazel Marie," my grandmother said. "I swear not to kidnap Lily or harm a hair on her head."

Tizzy crawled up my legs and was holding on to my head as if it were a giant acorn she had to protect. "Tell her, Lils. Tell her."

She nodded at the powerful witch, whom she apparently was on a first name basis with. "People keep telling me their truths. Some of these truths shouldn't be spoken. Frankly, I'm scared to talk to anyone. This kind of thing could get me in a lot of trouble on both sides of the fence in this town."

"You shouldn't have inherited Liliana's ability, but it seems this hellmouth has triggered your witch blood." She smiled and touched Lily's cheek. "I always knew our Lily was special. But now she's even more unique."

"Like a snowflake," Tizzy chimed in.

Our Lily? She was *my* Lily, not my grandmother's.

"How do I get rid of it?" Lily asked. "I won't be able to stay in Paradise Falls if I keep the ability. Extracting secrets from shifters is a quick way to get dead."

"Once it's triggered, there's no off switch." My grandmother gave Lily a sad smile. "If it's any consolation, it should lessen in potency if we can fix this gaping hole to hell."

My brave friend stepped around me and faced Clementine. "Well, then let's fix this gaping hole to hell?"

THE GRAND INQUISITOR HAD HER LACKEYS LINE UP ALL

the descendants of the original coven. Like a drill sergeant with her platoon, she walked up and down the line casting intimidating glares at each and every one of the thirty-one witches and warlocks.

I recognized several of them, including Mercy Langston, Jenny Weaver, Lena Ansel, her daughter Becksy, my officers Alice Michaels and John Parker, Romy Quinn, and Pierce Roberts. I prayed like crazy that Pierce Roberts was involved. I wanted to see the smug look leave his face when he got his comeuppance from our queen.

"Wait a minute," I said. I pulled the cards from my pocket. J. A. R. A. "Goddess, I'm dense." I gestured to the crowd. "I think I can narrow this down. Let's keep Jenny, John, Alice, Lena Ansel, Pierce Roberts, and Romy. Everyone else can go sit across the road and wait."

"What do you know, Hazel?" my dad asked.

"I think these cards carry the initials of the four people who brought back four ghost witches. J for John or Jenny, A for Alice or Ansel, one of the As is definitely for Agatha, and R is for Romy or Roberts. No one else has these as a first initial of their first or last name."

"Are you sure about this?"

I shook my head. "No, but it would be less taxing on Lily to deal with six people instead of thirty-one."

My dad nodded. He gestured to the men corralling the witches and warlocks and cut the six from the herd and sent the rest across the street.

Lily stood next to the Grand Inquisitor, and as they walked down the line a third time, she asked each one of them, "Did you take part in the summoning ritual?"

Lily started with Robert Pierce. I had my fingers and toes crossed. But, alas, he was innocent. At least of this crime. In my book, he was still guilty of being an asshole.

Romy Quinn was next. Lily sniffed her and gave me a quick nod. Romy broke down the moment Lily asked, and she confessed to being a part of a small coven. A rogue coven. The next one to confess was Jenny Weaver, the muffin lady. She didn't offer any resistance. Her and Romy sobbed as they kept apologizing.

Lily moved on to the last three people in line, Lena Ansel, my officer, John Parker, and Alice Michaels.

Lena Ansel said, "No, I had nothing to do with it." But when she asked John Parker, his face turned almost purple as he fought to hold his tongue.

"John?" He was a good cop. Why would he participate

in a coven? "I don't understand. What are you hiding?" There was no second J on the cards. Maybe I'd got the card idea wrong?

"It was never supposed to be like this," he said. His anger and fear made his words sharp and loud.

"What wasn't supposed to be like this?"

He lunged at me. I side-stepped his outstretched arms and put him down. He held up his hands, magic sparking from his fingertips.

"Don't do it, John. The magic is too unpredictable, especially at the edge of the hellmouth." I held up my hand to keep Ford and my dad away.

"Why did you partner me with a shifter?" John said, his voice almost broken.

"I don't understand. Were you part of the summoning, or is this about something else?"

"One week on patrol with Thomas and I got her scent." Tears pooled his eyes. "I'd been with Agatha for thirty years. We were happy. We were. Until you..." I looked across the way to where Mitzy Thomas stood. He shook his head. "Agatha's dead, and it's all my fault. She wouldn't have done this stupid ritual if I hadn't left her."

Oh Goddess, he and Mitzy had caught the mating

scent, but he'd been in a committed relationship. Crap. Hazel Kinsey ruining lives, one mating scent at a time. No wonder he'd been so angry.

I turned to Romy, who'd I'd always considered a friend. "Why? Why did you summon the dead witches and conjure a hellmouth in the middle of town?"

"We didn't mean to call up the hellmouth," Romy said. "Agatha...It was her idea. She said that the founding coven had figured out a spell to strengthen our magic, and it would have worked if the four hadn't died during the incantation. We just wanted them to finish the spell."

"To what end?" my grandmother asked.

"I just wanted more magic," Jenny said. She glanced at John. "But I think Agatha wanted enough power to break the mating scent."

I gulped as Agatha's desire hit me hard. "All this to get John back." Had it been my fault. I'm the one who'd insisted that shifters and witches pair up. There was one more person to ask. Alice Michaels. I stared at her. "You?" I asked.

She nodded. "We didn't mean for any of this to happen. We've been trying non-stop to reverse the spell, but nothing works."

"And Agatha?"

"The damn Tower card haunted us. Every scenario brought up the disaster card. Agatha tried to appease the angry ghosts with spells she'd cast on those stupid rubber legs. She'd nearly given Jenny and Romy heart attacks putting them near their places of business."

"How did she die?"

Tanya, who had arrived at some point, said, "Her heart exploded."

"It was those damn witches," Romy said.

"Which ones?" There seemed to be a lot of damn witches around here.

"The dead ones," Alice said. "I fear the rest of us are next."

"Don't you worry," the Grand Inquisitor said. "You'll be safe as kittens in my cells. Just ask my son."

My dad rolled his eyes, and for the first time, I could see a little of myself in him.

Grandma's security team sent the innocent witches and warlocks home with a promise of explanations. She also made sure each and every one of them knew that any magic use until the ban was lifted would result in jail time.

I stepped up to John Parker. "I'm sorry, John."

He wouldn't look at me. Ford chimed in. "The mate scent pairs those who are fated. It would have happened eventually, with or without Hazel putting you two together. This isn't her fault, and it's not yours or Mitzy's fault either."

"Do you love her?" I asked.

John looked at me, his eyes red and stark. "Goddess help me, I do."

I nodded. "What happened to Agatha is not your fault," I reiterated. I wished I could be so kind with myself, but the guilt was overwhelming. "Go work the line with Thomas. Your partner needs you."

John walked away, and I turned to my grandma. "Okay. We know the culprits. How do we fix this?" I waved my hand at the nauseating pit.

"We push the three of them into the hellmouth. It closes over them. Problem solved."

Romy and Jenny sobbed loudly now. Alice looked like her head would explode.

"I kid," said the Grand Inquisitor. "The portal to Hell would only feed off their stupidity.

Unexpectedly, Alice raised her fist and cried out, "*Macht, die, komm zu mir sein. Power to be, come to me!*"

The air around us blasted out in all directions like a sonic wave knocking everyone to the ground and shaking the street until every part of me rattled. I rolled onto my back and pushed myself up. Because the earlier explosion at Romy's had hurt my ribs, the effort caused a pinching pain in my lungs when I inhaled.

I scanned the area.

Ford was helping Lily to her feet. The Grand Inquisitor was checking over my father for injuries and most of her men were brushing debris from their clothes. No one was trying to catch the bad guys. I looked around for Alice. Where she'd been standing there was a big greasy red stain on the ground.

Ouch. Could it be that we had one less witch to worry about. I stared at Jenny and Romy who had huddled together for safety. Ford grabbed them by the backs of their shirts and hauled them to their feet.

Tizzy poked her head up from out of my large jacket pocket. "Holy shit, Haze!" she cried.

"What are you doing in there?" I asked.

"Hiding, of course?"

"What in the hell was that?" I said.

"That idiot tried to pull off the power spell by herself," my grandma said. She dusted her own clothes now that she'd assured herself that my dad was okay.

At that moment, four dark shadows, the ones I'd seen in the vision crawled out of the tarry hellmouth.

"She did it," Jenny Weaver cried out. She looked afraid, not triumphant. "She called the stricken ones."

"How do we put them back?" I asked.

Romy crab crawled backwards and said, "I don't know. We...I... I didn't think it would actually work."

The obsidian creatures stalked toward us like slow moving zombies. "We could probably run away. Will stabbing them in the head work?"

"It will take powerful magic to put them back in the ground," the Grand Inquisitor said.

"But we can't use magic here, or we'll feed the freaking door to the devil," Tizzy protested. "You already said, first rule of hellmouth. Don't feed the hellmouth."

"I'm pulling my power from across the country. If we join together, we might be able to stop the ghosts from completely entering this realm."

I looked at the gruesome ghouls, who, like slugs, were leaving a trail of slime behind them as they shambled toward us. Theirs faces contorted unnaturally, and I tried to suppress the horror rising in my gut. "They look pretty complete now."

"But they're not," she said with an irritation reserved for school marms and witch queens.

"What happens if your magic leaks into Paradise Falls?"

"Then you all will die."

"Uhm…"

"Don't worry," she said. "I'll be fine. I've survived worse."

"Oh, that's exactly what I was worried about."

"Hurry!" Grandmother said. "We need to join now."

I grabbed her hand, Lily came over and took her other. My father, Tanya, Jenny, Romy, and the security team all joined hands on the other side. Tizzy hugged my neck, and Ford, who had no magic except his love for me, took my hand.

"There's nothing here.

Not anymore.

Go back to sleep.

Go back you four."

I gave my grandmother an incredulous look.

"Chant!" she demanded.

We all repeated the ridiculous spell:

"There's nothing here.

Not anymore.

Go back to sleep.

Go back you four."

Over and over we said the words. The wind began to whip around us like a mini-cyclone, so fast and strong I could barely stay on my feet. Ford moved behind me and held me up. The wails coming from the abominations were akin to banshee screams. I kept chanting. We all kept chanting.

It wasn't working. They just kept coming toward us.

"We need a power focus," the Grand Inquisitor shouted. "Something to channel the magic through. It's too scattered because of the hellmouth."

Romy was crying, "This is all my fault. My fault." Her cat jumped down and started walking toward the gory used-to-be witches.

"No," Tizzy said. She leaped off my shoulder, her arms spread wide as she glided past the cat. "Use me!"

"Tisiphone!" I yelled.

But the Grand Inquisitor said the magic words once again:

"There's nothing here.

Not anymore.

Go back to sleep.

Go back you four."

Power smooshed us in the line together as white light shot out of The Grand Inquisitor's eyes, nose and mouth moving straight into my flying familiar and raining sunshine over the conjured spirits. They melted to the asphalt under the intense rays of magic.

In less than a blink, everything went dark and silent.

The horror I'd been holding back bubbled up in me like a cauldron full of pitch. I screamed, "Tizzy!"

She was lying in the street where the ghosts had disappeared. Unmoving. Goddess help me, she wasn't moving.

"Tiz!" I dropped to my knees, my legs weak with grief, and I scrabbled across the asphalt toward her. Lily and Ford were kneeling next to me as, carefully, I picked her up. I gasped. Her little body was so light. So vulnerable. I'd never seen her look so helpless. I cradled her gently against me. "Tiz." I shook her chest with my fingertip. "Tisiphone." Tears clouded my vision. "Lily, she's not breathing."

Lily, who'd studied medicine, if only informally, her entire adult life, took Tiz from me. She began chest compressions and blowing over her nose and mouth. Chaos exploded around us, but I couldn't care what was happening outside of Lily performing squirrel CPR. Instead, I prayed hard for the Goddess to bring her back. Ford held me as I rocked back and forth, my prayers getting more frantic with each second.

After a few minutes, Lily looked up at me, her face full of grief. "It's not working."

"Put her down," a sharp voice said. I brushed at my eyes. Loopyhead the cat was circling Lily's feet. "Put her down," she said again. "I know how to help her." If I didn't know better, I'd say she was worried. Frantic even.

Lily looked at me. A question in her expression.

The Grand Inquisitor said, "Let her try. Familiars have a different kind of magic. If anyone can save your Tisiphone, it might be Lupitia."

The fat cat sniffed around Tizzy after Lily placed her on the ground. My heart felt like a semi-truck had backed over it a dozen times. "Do something already," I told the terrible tabby.

Without a word of warning, Luchiapet pounced on top of my squirrel and, if she hadn't already stopped breathing, would have smothered her.

"What are you doing, you psychopathic feline?"

Lily grabbed my arm and kept me from turning the Persian cat into a Persian rug.

The cat from hell glowed neon green. Seconds later, we heard a squeak and wheeze. My heart pounded so hard I'd thought it would break a few more ribs as I dropped to my knees. Lu-puta casually removed herself from Tizzy. The squirrel blinked up at me, her eyes reflecting a myriad of emotions.

"Haze," she said. I pulled her into my arms. "What happened?"

"You died," I cried. "Don't you ever do that to me again!"

"Can I…" she said in a weak whisper.

"Can you what? You want some water? Some food? An increase in your allowance? Anything," I told her, unbelievably grateful to have her back. "You can have anything you want."

"I want..." She hacked and coughed. My lungs squeezed with guilt. "I want..." she said again.

"Tell me." I stroked my fingertip across her fuzzy cheek.

"I want a smoke machine, and eyeballs and guts, and cobwebs, and a coffin with a skeleton, oh, and a chain-saw. Minus the chain, of course."

My blood pressure ratcheted up several notches.

"You did say she could have anything," Lily said.

"*Et tu*, Lily?" I sighed. Heavily. "Fine. But you let me break it to Ford."

"Woo hooo!" Tizzy whipped around and fist pumped the air. "I win."

"You're awfully spry for being dead a few minutes ago."

"It's not the first time I died. I'm sure it won't be the last." She put a clenched paw on her hip. "I make old look good."

I knew I wasn't her first witch, but we never talked about her past, so sometimes I forgot she was hundreds, maybe even a thousand years old.

"You make cute look sinister."

"There's no denying it." She smiled, her cheeks puffing out. "I am adorable."

"Yes," I agreed then chuckled. "You really are." Our magic had gotten rid of the ghosts, but the hellmouth was still prominently featured in the middle of the intersection. "So," I said to Grandmother. "How do we get rid of the big, black, pit of doom?"

"Maybe we could gate it off and charge admission," Tizzy said

"It won't come to that," the Battle-axe said. "You were on the right track with the magic ban. Starve the hellmouth until after the blood moon, and it will close itself."

"So, we just ignore the gates to Hell in the middle of our town and just go about business as usual?"

"Pretty much," she said. She gave her men a whistle and circled her finger. "Round them up, boys. I have cells with their names on it."

Jenny didn't have her familiar with her, but Romy Quinn was hugging her foul cat so hard its eyes were bulging.

"Can Lupitia stay with us until Romy gets out of jail?" asked Tizzy.

"For goddess sake, why?"

"I love her," Tizzy said.

"No," I gasped. Not Ludoodiehead, anyone but her! Had that been the reason she'd thrown herself into the middle of danger. For love? "Romy could be gone for a hundred years, Tizzy. That's a long time to commit?"

"Do you think so?" Ford asked.

"Uhm, I only meant..." I pulled Tizzy off my shoulder, so I could look her in the eye. "When did this happen?"

Lupitachip jumped down from Romy's arms to the ground and answered for Tizzy. "We've been courting for two months now." She stared up at me and blinked her green eyes. "I love her, too."

"Goddess help me." I looked at Ford.

"Who are we to stand in the path of true love," the werebear said with just the barest hint of an amused smile.

"Har-har," I said. He was supposed to have my back.

"It seems you have things under control here, Hazel," the Grand Inquisitor said. "I'll be off now." Her men had already popped out with the prisoners, and I wondered if their transportation magic was feeding our evil hole. "I've shielded my magic from here," she told me. It'll be okay now that the ghosts are banished."

"Good to know."

"Call me if you have any problems."

"I will." But not if there were any other options available first, like dropping a nuclear warhead on the town and wiping it out.

Grandmother went to my father next. "Kent," she said.

"Mother," he replied.

"Until next time."

She turned her face for him and he placed a kiss on her cheek.

"Until next time," he said.

Lily, Ford, Dad, Tanya, Tizzy, and Stupid-Lupid loaded up in the vehicles. It was almost one o'clock now, and all I wanted was my soft, warm bed.

Grandmother asked me to hang back for a moment, and when it was just the two of us, she handed me a piece of paper.

There was a name written on it with an address for a town in Missouri. "What's this?"

"Don't tell Lily where you got the information. But I think it might be time for her to start a new life. A real life. Somewhere away from Paradise Falls."

And with those parting words, she sparkled out.

The past twenty-four hours had made me feel a little like Jack Bauer, and I was in serious need of a commercial break. I stared at the bubbly black entrance to Satan's palace and felt the weariness of responsibility weigh me down.

Ford honked the truck horn, and the pit farted at me all at the same time. I looked up at the sky. "Thank you, Goddess." As I walked to the truck, I gazed fondly at my family as they impatiently waited for me. "Thank you."

CHAPTER 15

I t was the day before Halloween, and the hole on Main Street was down to about the size of a beach ball. The witches and warlocks in town had gone on a strict magic diet, and as the Grand Inquisitor predicted, the hellmouth was closing on its own.

Ford's house hadn't fared nearly as well. Tizzy, Lily, and Loopydupie had turned the house into Dante's nine circles of Hell. The irony that our town had almost been a part of the first circle did not escape me. Ford's family joined our haunted house, including his little brother, and they were all coming over for a dinner party. A sort of pre-Haunted House celebration. I still didn't understand the distance between Ford and his baby bro, but it could have just been the age gap. Teenagers have many different perspectives than adults with full-time jobs and mortgages.

Anita Baylor, Ford's mom, was dressed in a witch costume, classic black pointy hat and black dress. She looked adorable. "Welcome, Nita." I took the whipped cream salad dessert from her. It had pistachio pudding, crushed pineapple, and pecans in it, and was one of my favorite dishes. Lincoln stood out front, his letter jacket buttoned up tight. He wore a pair of jeans that he rolled at the cuff. As he stood there, he reminded me so much of Ford at that age.

Ford was stringing up skeleton lights at the fence when a familiar honking startled him. A clown with big floppy pink shoes, a giant bow tie, and a fuzzy pink wig ran up to him, squeezed a bulb in its hand and water shot from the bow tie into Ford's face. The clown honked again and began running away.

However, a size fifty shoe cannot outrun a size thirteen, and Ford quickly managed to catch the clown and tackle it to the ground. A haze of glitter flew in the air as a distinctly female voice cried out.

Oh, crap. This clown was a girl.

"Get off her," Lincoln shouted. "Dude. Not cool."

Ford stood up and pulled the clown to her feet. He popped off the nose and pulled off the wig. "Becksy?"

Wow, the clown was the waitress from Lolo's.

Lincoln was extricating the teenage witch from his brother's grasp. He checked her over, a profoundly worried expression on his young face. "Are you okay?"

"I'm all right," she said, her eyes dreamily gazing into his.

"What the hell did you think you were doing?" Ford said, his anger still at the surface.

I realized exactly what was going on. I took Ford's arms. "Points to the witches." Thanks to the help of a smart shifter in love. I leaned into Ford's body. "I bet she smells like spring flowers to him, and he smells like peach pie." I smiled.

He looked startled for a moment and said, "You think?"

"Oh yeah," I said. Then to the teenagers I added, "Good one, Becksy." I suspected Lincoln and some of his other friends had been the previous two clowns. I winked at the teenager, a small part of me envying all the years they would have that I missed out on with Ford.

My father showed up with Tanya on his arm, and I was proud of how well I kept my gag reflex under control.

When I got a moment alone with Lily, I told her about

the name and address in a town called Moonrise, Missouri. Using the information Grandmother had given me, I'd done some groundwork. Turns out that Lily's uncle was alive. He'd moved away from Paradise Falls before she was born. I'd vetted him through my contacts at the FBI, carefully so as not to blow his life up. He'd moved around some, but he never caused problems anywhere he went. Lily's new ability was making her less than popular around Paradise Falls, and the small town where her uncle lived in Southern Missouri seemed like a great place for Lily to get a fresh start.

"His name is Daniel," I told her.

"You mean…"

"Yes, your brother was named for him. He must have meant a lot to your dad, even if they didn't keep in touch."

I hugged her, and we both cried a little. Lily for the loss of her brother and the possibility a new life would bring, and, me, because I was going to miss my best friend. It had been difficult to part with her seventeen years ago, but this time around, our goodbye would be even harder.

After we had all the finishing touches done on the haunted house, Ford put his arm around me. "We have a few hours until sundown. Can I show you something?"

"Sure," I said.

Tizzy, who happened to be close by said, "She's seen your ween before, bearface."

Blessedly, he ignored her. "Come on."

FORD DROVE US AROUND FOR TWENTY MINUTES. I THINK. Being sure with my eyes closed was hard.

"Don't peek," he said for the bazzilionth time.

"I'm not peeking!"

Soon, the truck rolled to a slow stop. "Keep 'em closed."

"I am."

I heard his door open and close, then my door opened, and he lifted me out of the truck. My heart fluttered in my chest. He set me down and turned me once and said, "Okay, open them."

I blinked. Then I blinked again. I was staring at Agatha Milan's Victorian house. But why? "What's this?"

"It's ours," Ford said from behind me. "Well, kind of. I

mean, there is still some particulars, contracts and such that need to be signed by both of us and such."

It had only been a week since Agatha died. "I don't understand."

"You loved this place. I saw it on your face."

"I do love this place, but how can we close so fast after the owner died, and how in the world can we afford this?"

"For one, this isn't a human town with human rules. Agatha left the house to John Parker, and he doesn't want it. And we can afford it because I was a bachelor for a long time. There wasn't a whole lot to spend my money on. And now I can do this for you. For us," he said. "It will be *our* home. And it will be filled with things that belong to us, not just me."

I stared at the gorgeous house for a moment then turned to face Ford and gasped. He was on one knee.

"I…"

He looked up at me, his blue eyes shining with purpose. "Hazel Marie Kinsey. You are sarcastic, mouthy, and a general pain in the ass."

I smirked even as the tears filled my eyes. "So romantic."

"But you are also vivacious, caring, wonderful, and beautiful. You are the love of my life. You make me happy. I never thought I'd have a chance at a life with you, my mate."

"This is more like it," I said, blinking back the tears.

He opened the velvet box in his hand, and the diamond ring looked full of stars. "Will you marry me?"

"You bought me a house. My dream house." My chest squeezed with joy. "I'd be a fool to say no."

"Is that a yes?"

"That's not only a yes, that's a hell to motherfluffin' yes."

He stood up and put the ring on my shaking finger.

"Do you have the keys?"

"Yeah," he said, "Why?"

I pressed my body to his and wiggled my hips against him. I yanked his head down and kissed him hard with the entire weight of my possession. He was mine. Ford Baylor was mine forever. When I let him up for air, I said, "I need the keys, because I want you to carry me across that threshold and bang my brains out over the hand carved oak banister. Then after, I'll suck your—"

"Haze!" my father shouted.

"What the…" I looked around and watched my dad, Anita, Baylor, Tizzy, Lucreature, Lily, Tanya, and Lincoln come out from hiding. Anita held a video camera and had it aimed at us.

"I'll erase that last bit," she said. "Congratulations."

"You could have warned me," I said to Ford through clenched teeth.

Ford grinned, his scent taking on a snickerdoodle aroma. "What were you saying about sucking—"

"You suck."

"As often as I can, darling." He picked me up in his arms. "As often as I can."

The End

PIT PERFECT MURDER

BARKSIDE OF THE MOON COZY MYSTERIES
BOOK 1

When cougar-shifter Lily Mason moves to Moonrise, Missouri, she wishes for only three things from the town and its human population. . . to find a job, to find a place to live, and to live as a human, not a therianthrope.

Lily gets more than she bargains for when a rescue pit bull named Smooshie rescues her from an oncoming car, and it's love at first sight. Thanks to Smooshie, Lily's first two wishes are granted by Parker Knowles, the owner of the Pit Bull Rescue center, who offers her a job at the shelter and the room over his garage for rent.

Lily's new life as an integrator is threatened when Smooshie finds Katherine Kapersky, the local church choir leader and head of the town council, dead in the field behind the rescue center. Unfortunately, there are more suspects than mourners for the elderly town leader. Can Lily keep her less-than-human status under wraps? Or will the killer, who has pulled off a nearly Pit Perfect murder, expose her to keep Lily and her dog from digging up the truth?

Chapter One

When I was eighteen years old, I came home from a sleepover and found my mom and dad with their throats cut, and their hearts ripped from their chests.

My little brother Danny was in a broom closet in the kitchen, his arms wrapped around his knees, and his face pale and ghostly. Until that day, I'd planned to go to college and study medicine after graduation, but instead, I ended up staying home and taking care of my seven-year-old brother.

Seventeen years later, my brother was murdered. At the time, Danny's death looked like it would go unsolved, much like my parents' had.

Without Haze Kinsey, my best friend since we were five, the killers would have gotten away with it. She was a special agent for the FBI for almost a decade, and when I called her about Danny's death, she dropped everything to come help me get him justice. The evil group of witches and Shifters responsible for the decimation of my family paid with their lives.

Yes. I said witches and Shifters. Did I forget to mention I'm a werecougar? Oh, and my friend Hazel is a witch. Recently, I discovered witches in my own family tree on my mother's side. Shifters, in general, only mated with Shifters, but witches were the exception. As a matter of fact, my friend Haze is mated to a bear Shifter.

I wouldn't have known about the witch in my genealogy, though, if a rogue witch coven hadn't done some funky hoodoo witchery to me. Apparently, the spell activated a latent talent that had been dormant in my hybrid genes.

My ancestor's magic acted like truth serum to anyone who came near her. No one could lie in her presence. Lucky me, my ability was a much lesser form of hers. People didn't have to tell me the truth, but whenever they were around me, they had the compulsion to overshare all sorts of private matters about themselves. This can get seriously uncomfortable for all parties involved. Like, the fact that I didn't need to know that Janet Strickland had been wearing the same pair of underwear for an entire week, or that Mike Dandridge had sexual fantasies about clowns.

My newfound talent made me unpopular and unwelcome in a town full of paranormal creatures who thrived on little deceptions. So, when Haze discovered the whereabouts of my dad's brother, a guy I hadn't known even existed, I sold all my belongings, let the bank have my parents' house, jumped in my truck, and headed south.

After two days and 700 miles of nonstop gray, snowy weather, I pulled my screeching green and yellow mini-truck into an auto repair shop called The Rusty Wrench. Much like my beloved pickup, I'd needed a new start, and moving to a small town occupied by humans seemed the best shot. I'd barely made it to Moonrise, Missouri before my truck began its death throes. The vehicle protested the last 127 miles by sputtering to a halt as I rolled her into the closest spot.

The shop was a small white-brick building with a one-car garage off to the right side. A black SUV and a white compact car occupied two of the six parking spots.

A sign on the office door said: *No Credit Cards. Cash Only. Some Local Checks Accepted (Except from Earl—You Know Why, Earl! You check-bouncing bastard).*

A man in stained coveralls, wiping a greasy tool with a rag, came out the side door of the garage. He had a full head of wavy gray hair, bushy eyebrows over light blue, almost colorless eyes, and a minimally lined face that made me wonder about his age. I got out of the truck to greet him.

"Can I help you, miss?" His voice was soft and raspy with a strong accent that was not quite Deep South.

"Yes, please." I adjusted my puffy winter coat. "The heater stopped working first. Then the truck started jerking for the last fifty miles or so."

He scratched his stubbly chin. "You could have thrown a rod, sheared the distributor, or you have a bad ignition module. That's pretty common on these trucks."

I blinked at him. I could name every muscle in the human body and twelve different kinds of viruses, but I didn't know a spark plug from a radiator cap. "And that all means…"

"If you threw a rod, the engine is toast. You'll need a new vehicle."

"Crap." I grimaced. "What if it's the other thingies?"

The scruffy mechanic shrugged. "A sheared distributor is an easy fix, but I have to order in the part, which means it won't get fixed for a couple of days. Best-case scenario, it's the ignition module. I have a few on hand. Could get you going in a couple of hours, but..." he looked over my shoulder at the truck and shook his head, "...I wouldn't get your hopes up."

I must've looked really forlorn because the guy said, "It might not need any parts. Let me take a look at it first. You can grab a cup of coffee across the street at Langdon's One-Stop."

He pointed to the gas station across the road. It didn't look like much. The pale-blue paint on the front of the building looked in need of a new coat, and the weather-beaten sign with the store's name on it had seen better days. There was a car at the gas pumps and a couple more in the parking lot, but not enough to call it busy.

I'd had enough of one-stops, though, thank you. The bathrooms had been horrible enough to make a wereraccoon yark, and it took a lot to make those garbage eaters sick. Besides, I wasn't just passing through Moonrise, Missouri.

"Have you ever heard of The Cat's Meow Café?" Saying the name out loud made me smile the way it had when Hazel had first said it to me. I'd followed my GPS into town, so I knew I wasn't too far away from the place.

"Just up the street about two blocks, take a right on Sterling Street. You can't miss it. I should have some news in about an hour or so, but take your time."

"Thank you, Mister…"

"Greer." He shoved the tool in his pocket. "Greer Knowles."

"I'm Lily Mason."

"Nice to meet ya," said Greer. "The place gets hoppin' around noon. That's when church lets out."

I looked at my phone. It was a little before noon now. "Good. I could go for something to eat. How are the burgers?"

"Best in town," he quipped.

I laughed. "Good enough."

Even in the sub-freezing temperature, my hands were sweating in my mittens. I wasn't sure what had me more nervous, leaving the town I grew up in for the first time in my life or meeting an uncle I'd never known existed.

I crossed a four-way intersection. One of the signs was missing, and I saw the four-by-four post had snapped off at its base. I hadn't noticed it on my way in. Crap. Had I run a stop sign? I walked the two blocks to Sterling. The diner was just where Greer had said. A blue truck, a green mini-coup, and a sheriff's SUV were parked out front.

An alarm dinged as the glass door opened to The Cat's Meow. Inside, there was a row of six booths along the wall, four tables that seated four out in the open floor, and counter seating with about eight cushioned black stools. The interior décor was rustic country with orange tabby kitsch everywhere. A man in blue jeans and a button-down shirt with a string tie sat in the nearest booth. A female police officer sat at a counter chair sipping coffee and eating a cinnamon roll. Two elderly women, one with snowball-white hair, the other a dyed strawberry-blonde, sat in a back booth.

The white poof-headed lady said, "This egg is not over-medium."

"Well, call the mayor," said Redhead. "You're unhappy with your eggs. Again."

"See this?" She pointed at the offending egg. "Slime, right here. Egg snot. You want to eat it?"

"If it'll make you shut up about breakfast food, I'll eat it and lick the plate."

A man with copper-colored hair and a thick beard, tall and well-muscled, stepped out of the kitchen. He wore a white apron around his waist, and he had on a black T-shirt and blue jeans. He held a plate with a single fried egg shining in the middle.

The old woman with the snowy hair blushed, her thin skin pinking up as he crossed the room to their table. "Here you go, Opal. Sorry 'bout the mix-up on your egg." He slid the plate in front of her. "This one is pure perfection." He grinned, his broad smile shining. "Just like you." He winked.

Opal giggled.

The redhead rolled her eyes. "You're as easy as the eggs."

"Oh, Pearl. You're just mad he didn't flirt with you."

As the women bickered over the definition of flirting, the cook glanced at me. He seemed startled to see me there. "You can sit anywhere," he said. "Just pick an open spot."

"I'm actually looking for someone," I told him.

"Who?"

"Daniel Mason." Saying his name gave me a hollow ache. My parents had named my brother Daniel, which told me my dad had loved his brother, even if he didn't speak about him.

The man's brows rose. "And why are you looking for him?"

I immediately knew he was a werecougar like me. The scent was the first clue, and his eyes glowing, just for a second, was another. "You're Daniel Mason, aren't you?"

He moved in closer to me and whispered barely audibly, but with my Shifter senses, I heard him loud and clear. "I go by Buzz these days."

"Who's your new friend, Buzz?" the policewoman asked. Now that she was looking up from her newspaper, I could see she was young.

He flashed a charming smile her way. "Never you mind, Nadine." He gestured to a waitress, a middle-aged woman with sandy-colored hair, wearing a black T-shirt and a blue jean skirt. "Top off her coffee, Freda. Get Nadine's mind on something other than me."

"That'll be a tough 'un, Buzz." Freda laughed. "I don't think Deputy Booth comes here for the cooking."

"More like the cook," the elderly lady with the light strawberry-blonde hair said. She and her friend cackled.

The policewoman's cheeks turned a shade of crimson that flattered her chestnut-brown hair and pale complexion. "Y'all mind your P's and Q's."

Buzz chuckled and shook his head. He turned his attention back to me. "Why is a pretty young thing like you interested in plain ol' me?"

I detected a slight apprehension in his voice.

"If you're Buzz Mason, I'm Lily Mason, and you're my uncle."

The man narrowed his dark-emerald gaze at me. "I think we'd better talk in private."

Want more? Got to
www.barksideofthemoonmysteries.com

PARANORMAL MYSTERIES & ROMANCES

BY RENEE GEORGE

Witchin' Impossible Cozy Mysteries

www.witchinimpossible.com

Witchin' Impossible (Book 1)

Rogue Coven (Book 2)

Familiar Protocol (Booke 3)

Mr & Mrs. Shift (Book 4)

Barkside of the Moon Mysteries

www.barksideofthemoonmysteries.com

Pit Perfect Murder (Book 1)

Murder & The Money Pit (Book 2)

The Pit List Murders (Book 3)

Peculiar Mysteries

www.peculiarmysteries.com

You've Got Tail (Book 1) FREE Download

My Furry Valentine (Book 2)

Thank You For Not Shifting (Book 3)

My Hairy Halloween (Book 4)

In the Midnight Howl (Book 5)

My Peculiar Road Trip (Magic & Mayhem) (Book 6)

Furred Lines (Book7)

My Wolfy Wedding (Book 8)

Who Let The Wolves Out? (Book 9)

Madder Than Hell

www.madder-than-hell.com

Gone With The Minion (Book 1)

Devil On A Hot Tin Roof (Book 2)

A Street Car Named Demonic (Book 3)

ABOUT THE AUTHOR

I am a USA Today Bestselling author who writes paranormal mysteries and romances because I love all things whodunit, Otherworldly, and weird. Also, I wish my pittie, the adorable Kona Princess Warrior, and my beagle, Josie the Incontinent Princess, could talk. Or at least be more like Scooby-Doo and help me unmask villains at the haunted house up the street.

When I'm not writing about mystery-solving were-cougars or the adventures of a hapless psychic living among shapeshifters, I am preyed upon by stray kittens who end up living in my house because I can't say no to those sweet, furry faces. (Someone stop telling them where I live!)

I live in Mid-Missouri with my family and I spend my non-writing time doing really cool stuff...like watching TV and cleaning up dog poop.

Printed in Great Britain
by Amazon